D0192657

'[illegible] is brilliant now to see [illegible]
[illegible] te-deep morality, it [illegible]
not sure I know another [illegible]
and so full of longing, so [illegible]
[illegible] atifying in its candour. [illegible]
[illegible] ng the best novels I [illegible]
[illegible] nonce abroad'

[illegible] ere is a sly, beguiling [illegible]
[illegible] eeling for me the [illegible]
[illegible] peare. MacKenzie is not [illegible]
[illegible] e's already there'

'[illegible] eautiful, [illegible]
[illegible] ng [illegible]
[illegible] s cad reminded me [illegible]
[illegible] se is stunning'

[illegible] illiant. A pervasive sense [illegible]
[illegible]
[illegible]

[illegible] intelligent and [illegible]
[illegible] life of a foreigner whose own [illegible]
[illegible] with the tensions [illegible]
[illegible] el climaxes [illegible]

‘This brilliant novel has no time for platitudes or conventional, ankle-deep morality; it plunges us straight to the depths. I’m not sure I know another book that feels at once so disaffected and so full of longing, so expansive in its sympathy and so terrifying in its candour. Devastating, funny and wise, it’s among the best novels I know about the fate of American innocence abroad’ GARTH GREENWELL

‘There is a sly, brooding intelligence at work in this novel, recalling for me the startling, highest times in American literature. MacKenzie is not just a great writer in the making – he’s already there’ BRAD WATSON

‘A beautiful, wry and honest exploration of belonging and not-belonging. The sharpness and precision with which the story is told reminded me in parts of Maggie Nelson … the prose is stunning’ SOPHIE MACKINTOSH

‘Brilliant. A pervasive sense of unrest, both large and small scale, social and personal, [is] conveyed in MacKenzie’s unruffled, discerning prose. MacKenzie has captured one of the most memorable narrative voices in recent fiction’
Publishers Weekly

‘Intelligent and atmospheric, *Feast Days* deftly limns the inner life of a foreigner whose own trajectory becomes increasingly bound up with the tensions and complexities of the society in which she has landed’ CHLOE ARIDJIS

‘Poignant and perceptive’ *Booklist*

‘The novel of the ugly American living abroad has bloomed into a genre all its own … Charles Portis’s *Gringos*, Ben Lerner’s *Leaving the Atocha Station*, Nell Zink’s *The Wallcreeper* … Ian MacKenzie’s second novel arrives as a worthy addition to that list’ *New York Times*

‘A story about love and power, luxury and empire, set in one of the most socially stratified countries on the planet. MacKenzie’s slender novel feels heavier than many novels twice its weight’ *San Francisco Chronicle*

ALSO BY IAN MACKENZIE

City of Strangers

FEAST DAYS

IAN MACKENZIE

4th ESTATE • *London*

4th Estate
An imprint of HarperCollins*Publishers*
1 London Bridge Street
London SE1 9GF
www.4thEstate.co.uk

First published in Great Britain in 2018 by 4th Estate
First published in the United States in 2018 by Little, Brown and Company, a division of Hachette Book Group, Inc.

1

A catalogue record for this book is available from the British Library.

ISBN 978-0-00-829854-8

Printed and bound in Great Britain by
CPI Group (UK) Ltd, Croydon

MIX
Paper from
responsible sources
FSC® C007454

This book is produced from independently certified FSC paper to ensure responsible forest management.

For more information visit: www.harpercollins.co.uk/green

For Kelsey—

first reader of everything,

fixes the mistakes no one else has to see

"Oh," I said, putting my hat on. "Oh."

—*Mark Strand,*
"I Will Love the Twenty-first Century"

PER DIEM

My husband worked for a bank in São Paulo, a city that reminded you of what Americans used to think the future would look like—gleaming and decrepit at once. The protests began in late spring, although, this being the Southern Hemisphere, it was really the fall. I was a young wife.

So. We were Americans abroad. We weren't the doomed travelers in a Paul Bowles novel, and we weren't the idealists or the malarial, religion-damaged burnouts in something by Greene; but we were people far from home nevertheless. Our naivety didn't have political consequences. We had G.P.S. in our smartphones. I don't think we were alcoholics. Our passports were in the same drawer as our collection of international adapters, none of which seemed to fit in Brazilian wall sockets. My husband was in the chrysalis stage of becoming a rich man, and idealism was never my vice.

Our tribe was an anxious tribe. This was after Lehman Brothers, Fannie Mae and Freddie Mac, after Occupy—people were starting to talk about the economic crisis in the past tense, boxing it up in the language of history. The Great Recession. The name was something we needed. I was amazed by how fragile wealthy men seemed in their own eyes. They could be thin-skinned also, mistrustful, myopic, boastful, cowardly, and frequently sanctimonious. Call it the anxiety of late capitalism. I should say that it was my husband who belonged to this tribe. I was ancillary—a word that comes from the Latin for "having the status of a female slave." That's the sort of thing I know, and it tells you something about how I misspent my education. The term among expats for people like me was "trailing spouse."

I wasn't aware until after living there for some time that São Paulo lies almost exactly on the Tropic of Capricorn. The city was a liminal place, not quite tropical, not quite subtropical—really, it was both things at once. This fact, when I discovered it, possessed a kind of explanatory force.

One night we went to the Reserva Cultural to see the new Coen brothers film, about a folksinger in Greenwich Village in the 1960s who fails to become Bob Dylan, and afterward we walked up Avenida Paulista, past the radio antenna that from a distance resembled an ersatz Eiffel Tower, to a restaurant in Consolação. All the magazines liked it, a pretty restaurant on a bad corner. Nearby there were buildings covered with skins of stale graffiti, boarded-up windows, decaying brick, that sort of thing. I saw drug addicts in flagrante delicto. It wasn't uncommon in São Paulo to find high-end dining in the midst of ruin. The whole thing could have been an art installation about gentrification: *High-End Dining in the Midst of Ruin*. On the sidewalk I saw the froth of old garbage, blown around by city wind.

Inside the restaurant you were assaulted by tastefulness. The click of ice in a steel shaker, a curl of white staircase. The walls were stacked cubes of smoked glass. My husband said the chef was famous.

"Apparently this used to be a dive bar," he said. "Caetano Veloso and Chico Buarque used to come here."

"Those are co-workers of yours?"

"No, singers."

"Oh," I said.

"What?"

"You're doing Facts About Brazil again."

The men wore shirts with open collars. The women wore as little as possible. The bartender, a skinny black tie. The menu bragged of steak tartare, ceviche, gnocchi, gourmet mini-hamburgers. Whatever it was, it wasn't a dive bar anymore.

We ate out in São Paulo. Restaurantgoing was the local cult, and we got involved. A home-cooked meal, as a solution to the problem of sustenance, would have set off alarms—who made this? That makes us sound terrible, perhaps, and unable to look after ourselves, but it isn't an exaggeration.

This was around the time I stopped thinking of New York as back home. I told myself this meant I was officially an expatriate. My husband's transfer to São Paulo had come about almost entirely because he already spoke some Portuguese—college girlfriend, five semesters. We'd been in São Paulo six months already, and we might stay on for years. The adventure was open-ended. Everything depended on my husband's job; on variables outside my control, on events that hadn't happened yet. One of the first words I learned in Portuguese was the term for the fine rain that fell constantly in that city, something between drizzle and mist. I was blonde, slim hips. I liked to wear green clothes. At night the city had an electric chartreuse glow. I saw more dark windows than lighted ones in the concrete faces of apartment towers. I saw Brazilian flags, soccer matches playing endlessly on flat-screen televisions, traffic signals changing at empty intersections.

"So, in this scenario."

"In this scenario."

"In this scenario we wouldn't even be here."

"Or there would be a nanny. A professional caregiver."

"I meant we wouldn't be here in Brazil."

"People have children in Brazil," he said.

"But it would be different."

"It would be different."

"Because there would be this small creature with us all the time."

"You remain skeptical."

I laughed. "In a word," I said.

The waiter interrupted us to ask, in English, if we were enjoying the meal. When he went away I could see that my husband was annoyed. He felt it was an insult to his Portuguese, since he had used Portuguese earlier with the same waiter. I was sure the waiter only wanted to practice his English. It was perhaps fair to say that both men wanted to show off. "He was being polite," I said. "I know," my husband said.

São Paulo was a metropolitan area of twenty-one million people, and always in the throes of something. There were rumors of drought. There were gangland killings, labor strikes. Carjackings. Whole bus yards mysteriously went up in flames a couple of times a year—that was a thing. Criminals used dynamite to blast open A.T.M.s. Drinking water was delivered to our door in twenty-liter plastic jugs, and Brazil was making preparations to host the World Cup. The term of art was *megaevent*. "We're not ready," said the Brazilians I knew. I wondered if you could classify war as a megaevent. São Paulo was a megacity. Information began to accumulate. I was told things. I personally knew only rich Brazilians, because of my husband's job. But all Brazilians took such delight, perplexing to an American, in criticizing their country; it was a style of critique that managed to deprecate nation and self at once. They would break into spontaneous arias of complaint. Everybody did this—taxi drivers, dentists. The reservoirs were low, politicians were corrupt, the economy was failing. The levels that should have been rising were falling and the levels that should have been falling were rising. Taxes—taxes were high. I read in the newspaper that the police murdered more people than the criminals did. Everything in that city was intimately juxtaposed—favela and high-rise, crack dealer and opera house.

I saw a favela on a souvenir coffee mug before seeing one in person, and recognized instantly that the mosaic of crowded bright rectangles signified the makeshift roofs and walls of poor people's homes, such an image having become global visual shorthand for the shantytowns of the third world's developing urban gargantuas. Tourists bought the coffee mugs because apparently there was something heartwarming about aestheticizing squalor. Poverty was colorful. The middle class was said to be "emerging": a moving target. As soon as you get a bit of money, the things you once tolerated become intolerable.

When wealthy Brazilians left the country on vacation, they didn't visit museums, or do anything cultural, as far as I could tell. They shopped. They shopped for clothes and perfume, for smartphones, for children's toys.

In New York, I'd had a job in the public relations department of a multinational cement company. I wrote content for the company's Facebook page and Twitter feed—a cement company with a Twitter feed. It paid as well as you would imagine. My husband used to suggest I do a master's. He couldn't say in what. I was twenty-five years old on the day of our wedding, an age when the future still seemed to shape itself willingly around whatever decisions I made. "With your degree," said my unmarried friends—who were most of my friends—as if marriage somehow precluded the rest of life. But that degree wasn't doing much for me. And I loved my husband. Something hadn't jelled for me after college, professionally, and because I married early, because my husband made money, I was able to get away with it. "A woman without a job actually *is* like a fish without a bicycle," as a friend of mine put it. "I'm not sure that makes sense," I said. "Well, you have to imagine the fish looking really sad about not having the bicycle," my friend said.

And so the prospect of living abroad initially had a primal, precognitive appeal—*Brazil!* I wrote the country's name on A.T.M. receipts, cocktail napkins, Con Ed bills. We talked about what I could do there. It seemed like a chance to press the reset button. My husband, with the idea that I might write a blog, made the case that life in a foreign country automatically conferred interest. "You have the right sense of humor for that kind of thing," he said. "And we could always have a kid," he said.

We made love the night before leaving America and then lay in bed, at the hotel the bank was paying for, sharing a bottle of Gevrey-Chambertin and adding up all the relocation expenses the bank was also paying for. I wrote everything on the inside cover of the novel I was reading—*Operation Shylock*, in which Philip Roth discovers that someone named Philip Roth is causing increasing amounts of trouble in Israel—and then we both stared, mesmerized, now with more anxiety than excitement: it looked like a list of debts.

Once upon a time I had the idea of doing translation work, of making that my career, but "translation work" turns out to be a contradiction in terms, unless you know Chinese and want to translate technical manuals.

So we moved to Brazil. And that night, at the restaurant that used to be a dive bar, we ate too much; we drank too much. The chef was famous. The meal was expensive. My husband, reviewing the bill, said: "The bank's paying for our flight home at Christmas." It was a private joke now—any time we spent money, we recalled something the bank was paying for. If we dined out after my husband returned from a business trip elsewhere in Brazil, he would say: "Per diem." As we left the restaurant and passed the maître d', my husband said, "Valeu." It was what people said after a meal. It meant: *Worth it.*

They came out of nowhere. They—three of them, boys. They hadn't come out of nowhere, of course, but we didn't see them until it was too late. "O.K.? O.K.?" the boy who was holding a knife in my face said.

The security people at the bank had given a briefing during our first week. The man who spoke was short, ridiculously muscled, ex-police. Something he said lodged in memory: You have to remember it's a transaction; you want to end it as fast as possible. My husband and I joked that the briefing should have been called "The Seven Habits of Highly Effective Robbery Victims."

Two boys worked on my husband—wallet, watch, phone. They searched his pockets by hand. Later, I thought of one's helplessness during a medical examination. They told us what to do, how to behave, and we obeyed. The boy with the knife pulled the strap of my purse over my head. He had bloodshot eyes, wrists like old rope; he couldn't have been more than nineteen.

"Aliança," one of the other boys said. He meant my husband's wedding band; I usually left mine at the apartment, on the advice of the ex-policeman. They were favela boys, dressed raggedly, seething with adrenaline and desperation. It was lucky for the boys that my husband spoke Portuguese—or lucky for my husband, or lucky for me. No foreigner without Portuguese would have known the meaning of "aliança."

Luck—the part of life you don't control. Or: you make your own luck. I can see both sides of that one.

The boy with the knife went through my husband's wallet and took out the cash. He wasn't satisfied. He threw the wallet to the pavement. "Tem mais," he said. It meant: *You have more*.

He put his hand on my shoulder. I was now a prop in the argument he was having with my husband; he gestured with the knife between my husband and me, saying things I didn't understand. While this was happening my mind was silent, empty. I didn't scream. I nodded when words were spoken in my direction. When I thought of it later, my mind ran to the safety of cliché. I was petrified. My heart was in my throat. But it was already a cliché: poor, dark-skinned street kids robbing rich, white-skinned foreigners—it was a script other people had performed on countless nights before this. Two of the boys were suddenly moving away with my husband, taking him somewhere, leaving me and the one boy alone. "O.K.?" he said to me. "O.K.?" I was scared out of my mind.

You heard stories in São Paulo of robberies that went badly. People were killed. People who resisted what was happening, people who were too slow to hand over the car keys, people who failed to follow the script. That was the ex-policeman's first piece of advice regarding the habits of highly effective robbery victims. Don't resist.

The lights of a car blazed suddenly across the boys' thin bodies. The sound of tires, other voices. It was enough to spook them. They ran. As he turned, the boy with the knife shoved me, and I fell to the ground. I closed my eyes and took a breath. I heard the sound of cheap plastic clapping on stone, going the other way, flip-flops.

My husband was there, lifting me, hugging my body to his. "I didn't think," he said.

I could see the light of the restaurant's door, people going in and out, in sight of where we just were robbed. I was empty. I could have stood in the same spot forever, empty. Moments ago we had been paying a check.

"You were leaving," I said.

"They were taking me to an A.T.M. They wanted me to take out more money," he said.

"Then what would have happened?"

The next day we went to a police station. I knew at once there was no point. The city was too large, and there were too many boys, too much everything. My husband told the story, made a report. They asked him to provide a list of what was stolen. Wallet, brown, leather, brand unknown. Purse, black, leather, Dolce & Gabbana. Men's watch, Burberry. Mobile phone, Samsung. Digital camera, Nikon. Cash, amount unknown. Wedding band, gold.

I wrote to Helen. Within hours, she wrote back:

> That sounds god-awful. Of course I imagine they were black, and I imagine this somehow makes you feel worse

about what happened. Don't. Don't think about it one more second.

Helen had also left New York during the previous year. She had a different set of reasons and went to Washington—a job, putting distance between herself and an ex-boyfriend, a general hunger that she had. Helen was my Republican friend. She said and thought things I would never say and rarely thought. She possessed a kind of Ayn Rand ruthlessness that troubled me but which I also admired. I replied:

Only one of the boys was black.

The cement vastness of São Paulo, seen from above, was otherworldly. Overgrown crops of high-rise condominiums extended endlessly under a pale yellow haze of polluted air, towers nuzzled together with tombstone snugness. Our neighborhood was south of Parque Ibirapuera, new money. The money aged as you went north; and then, farther north, the money disappeared. Poverty radiated outward to the edges of the city. At some point, driving around São Paulo, you crossed from the first world into the third world. Sometimes this happened in the space of a single block. Everywhere they were putting up more luxury high-rise condos, crushing to dust older buildings that had outlived their usefulness to the rich. I saw beggars and drug addicts going in and out of decaying structures in the last days before demolition. *Creative destruction*—that's the polite way we have of putting it now.

The building we lived in was called Maison Monet. That delicate name belied the reality that it was a fortress. You passed through two locking gates at the entrance. There were cameras in the garage, in the elevators. At night, an armed guard, always well-dressed. The building had twenty-eight stories of floor-through apartments, a pool, a phalanx of doormen. The penthouse and its residents were a mystery; I never saw anyone push the button for the top floor. The features of the building were the product of fear, a set of fears that New Yorkers generally didn't have anymore; New York had been tamed, but São Paulo was hairy with crime. We heard stories of apartment invasions, teams of men with guns. Men with guns swept through restaurants, hotels, they took everything. I thought about this every time I left the apartment, and the fact that I thought about it, that I was now a person who imagined the worst, bothered me more than the fear itself. The bank subsidized our apartment in São Paulo so that it cost no more than what our apartment in New York had cost, a difference of almost a thousand dollars a month. Here was one measure of my husband's professional value.

I was able to track my husband's phone over the Internet. There it was: a dot on the map, in a far northern zone of the city, impoverished and intimidating. I showed my husband. "Whoever that is, it's not those kids," he said. "And I already filed the insurance claim." I zoomed in, and the digital map approached the limit of its resolution. The dot—an exact, real-time location, complete with geocoordinates—seemed like a promise, but I had the feeling that if I were to physically move toward it, it would simply move away from me.

We told our Brazilian friends about the robbery. Everyone cooed with sympathy and recognition: it was as if we had passed some test of admission. "They normally rob you with guns in São Paulo," Marcos said. "Rio is knives," Iara said. We laughed. They had stories of their own. Crime was a source of anxiety among the upper classes in São Paulo. Until you became so rich that you literally flew everywhere by helicopter.

At dinner, a conversation about money. Brazil's economy, the mess it was in. Everything had gone so well for so long—and now the forecast was disaster. Our friends blamed the president, the party. Marcos worked with my husband and was married to Iara, and they knew João from somewhere. It was difficult to become friends with Brazilians—someone would suggest a time and not a place or a place and not a time—but after several months we were somehow still going to dinner with these people. They never laughed when they talked about politics.

Food appeared in portions so small they looked decorative, zoned on white plates, squares of black slate. Each plate-thing was accompanied by a lecture from the waiter: the per-dish speaking time was almost equal to the per-dish eating time. This was the tasting, the degustação. I didn't make an effort to understand when the waiter talked; I wanted to know as little as possible about what I was putting in my mouth, to be totally unprepared. I wanted no context. In some cases, I couldn't tell what the ingredients were, even after chewing and swallowing. *Degust* and *disgust* have the same root—*gustare*, to taste—but opposite meanings. *Ignorance*: that's the word for what I wanted.

Dinner with Brazilians—the first courses arrived at the table after nine o'clock. We ate alien forms from the sea, Galician octopus, slate-pencil urchins, a funny-looking gratin of salt cod. This chef was famous, too, a woman. Late in the evening, she emerged from the kitchen, observed by the diners, admired, radiating gentle authority. She was young, roughly my age. People went to her, and she received her guests like an ambassador, calm and generous. We ate suckling pig. We ate pastes and jellies and cold soups made from native Brazilian fruits. I couldn't disguise my dislike of certain things. My husband talked about every dish as if he were making notes for a review. Since moving to São Paulo, he had become one of those gastro-creeps. Food, as a subject for conversation, was for me on par with pornography. I wished that for him food were more like pornography: something to be enjoyed privately and not discussed as if it were art. I'm sure there is such a thing as better pornography and worse pornography, but you aren't supposed to go on about it.

And we ordered the wine pairings, of course. My husband insisted on this, as if in life one thing were always destined to be paired with another. I had as little interest in talking about the wine as I had in talking about the food, but I enjoyed drinking it. The waiters were happy to top off the glass of whatever they had just poured and I had just finished, gratis. "I'm having the wine pairing with the wine pairing," I said.

João was talking about soccer and asked my husband something about the rules of American football. My husband was in love with speaking Portuguese. I followed the conversation with more success than I participated in it, and I wondered if this made our Brazilian friends think of me as someone who was quiet, who let her husband do the talking. We draw our power from language. You aren't yourself in a foreign tongue. I can see why some people find this liberating.

I preferred to learn Portuguese by reading the newspapers. In the written language I could decode a number of words from their similarity to French. Live conversation was altogether different; I often found myself plunging into a state of zombielike incomprehension. Learning a language is a nonlinear affair. A moment of triumph often follows a crisis of confidence. Or else, after days of utter mastery, as your brain processes the language without that laborious sensation of actually processing it, you might find yourself suddenly suffering from language panic, total verb collapse, making errors of conjugation like someone blindfolded striking at tennis balls. You reach for a preposition from the shelf in your mind and find nothing there, absolutely nothing, no language whatsoever.

There had been a news event that day. Members of a homeless-rights group were occupying an unused building owned by a telecom giant. In Portuguese, the occupation was called an "invasion." Police blasted the occupiers out with water cannons; there were injuries. João was the one who mentioned it. He disapproved, but at first I misunderstood the source of his disapproval—the actions not of the police but of the homeless-rights group.

Marcos concurred: The government *tolerates* these people, he said. They let them do this business. Eventually they use the police, but for political reasons they don't arrest anyone after it is over. It is illegal what these people do. It is a kind of theft to use a building that doesn't belong to you. In the world, there is legal and illegal, there is not some third thing.

Iara spoke, his wife. "The only time a Brazilian will wait at a red light is when there is a camera," she said. She spoke in English; she wanted me to appreciate her point. "In America, even in the middle of the night, you wait at the red lights. Marcos never waits at the red lights."

Iara, I had loved her at once, she had a taste for irony. Her life had a vague glamour. She knew artists. She seemed to belong professionally to the gallery circuit of São Paulo without, as far as I could tell, actually making any money at it. That was the sort of thing that impressed me.

I heard tales of killings in our neighborhood. A kid who was closing up a café at the end of the night, shot by a robber. Three guys, connected guys, executed as they left a nondescript restaurant where they went for whiskey and cigars once a week; maybe a gambling debt. This happened just up the street. One of the doormen told me the next day as I was coming back to the apartment. The killers shot only the men they were trying to shoot, men they had reason to kill; they even warned off a waiter before opening fire. This information, when the doorman offered it, was intended to reassure me.

I spent a lot of time inside the apartment. I didn't have much of a choice. Even if I'd spoken Portuguese well enough, and even if there had been something for me to do, professionally, I didn't have the right kind of visa. I was a double major, cultural anthropology and dead languages. I was a net loss, in the idiom of my husband's industry. Or maybe I was a write-off. Housewife—I couldn't bring myself to use the word. Nor could my husband, I noticed. There really wasn't anywhere pleasant to walk.

"If I'd had a gun, I would have shot him in the head."

This was late, he couldn't sleep.

"You've never fired a gun in your life. You make fun of gun nuts."

"He was holding a knife in your face. I wish I'd had the power at that moment to kill him."

"No, you don't. Then you would have killed someone."

"My wife's face," my husband said.

What I did was look into other people's homes. I had a name for it: *The Life of Observation.*

The glassy apartment buildings started to resemble aquariums. My neighbors floated around inside their aquariums, lifting babies, carrying bowls, watching T.V. They all had giant flat-screen televisions. I knew because I could see them: I could watch what they were watching. For important soccer matches they put out flags. By neighbors I mean the people who lived in nearby buildings—about the people who lived in our building, above us and below us, I knew little, only what could be inferred from the bump of children overhead or a moment of close-quarters elevator interaction. The servant class—housekeepers, nannies, dog walkers, cooks—spent much more waking time in the apartments than their employers did. From our balcony, sixteen stories above the ground, we had some enviable sight lines. Unobstructed, cinematic views of distant street corners, newsstands and pharmacies, the roofs and exposed white bellies of other apartment buildings, swimming pools, bedroom windows a half mile away; it was a sniper's heaven. I didn't shoot anyone. Instead I sat on the sofa, in the middle of my glass-wrapped living room, like an object in a vitrine, reading. The blades of a helicopter occasionally chopped around the air outside. When I grew bored, I tried reading in a different room, and soon ran out of rooms.

The living room windows gave a view of the flight path into the domestic airport. If I stood at the window for several minutes, I would see a plane making its final descent. I remembered noticing the sound of the planes when we first moved in, but my awareness of it had faded over time. I sometimes caught the scent of jet fuel's hard cologne in the air.

Once a week a woman named Fabiana came to the apartment and gave me a Portuguese lesson. Cognates interested me because they were easy; I even invented cognates: "temptação," for instance, or "boastar." It was like rolling dice: once in a while I got what I wanted. "Aspiração" means what you think it means; so does "decadência." But Fabiana knew what I was up to. She would flash a tragic look that said: You must stop believing you can get away with this. Fabiana herself had good, sturdy English, dry and smooth, with an accent almost like a Frenchwoman's; it was the kind of accent that was paid for. Even her errors were perfect. Is it redundant to say that I saw price tags everywhere? I couldn't remember if this had started because of my husband, or earlier.

"I work in finance," my husband would say whenever someone asked about his job. He never said, "I'm an investment banker," let alone gave the name of his bank. He was like a doctor who says, "I work in medicine." Like a lifeguard who says, "I work in beaches." I came to believe he used this formulation because he liked the mystery of it; he capitalized on enigma. You either knew what he meant or you didn't. Secrets are important to men. Every man tells himself he could have been a spy in another life.

I was a part of this world by virtue of being my husband's wife. It shouldn't have been so; I never had the disposition to make money. I didn't study the right things, I didn't earn it—although you weren't really supposed to ask who earned what, who deserved. Now I was used to it, more or less, but at first the transition into my husband's world seemed sudden. It was as if I had been sucked up a column of light into the belly of the mothership, abducted into wealth. I acquired new habits, expectations of the world. We took taxis at two a.m. instead of waiting in putrid, silent tunnels for the train. We ordered wine by the bottle instead of the glass. I stopped adding up the price of a meal as I ate and instead simply enjoyed it. That's the thing about having money: there isn't necessarily more happiness, but there's so much more enjoyment. I honestly hadn't known that.

My husband often worked late. It was both in his nature and in the nature of his work. I had never watched so much television in my life. Against my will, I learned the rules of soccer.

The tracking software was still able to locate my husband's phone. This was four days after the robbery. The dot hadn't moved an inch. It was in Zona Norte, a place I wouldn't normally visit; a place others would discourage me from visiting. I looked up the street view of the address. It appeared to be a little bar, a boteco. I imagined a fat man running a side business out of the back, phones and watches that boys stole from people like me and my husband and then brought to him. I knew it was only a matter of time before the dot vanished.

The taxi driver was skeptical when I gave him the address but agreed to take me. Because of the distance from where I lived, he would earn a large fare.

Avenida 23 de Maio. High concrete walls sprayed with graffiti and coated in shadow; boys on motorcycles pulsing through veins of space between cars in otherwise congealed traffic. I saw a woman on the back of a moto, one arm around the driver's stomach, purse clutched to her side. She was dressed for work.

I saw none of the condominiums I was used to, the towers. Instead there were little houses, aluminum fences, all of it cheaply and quickly made and now carelessly painted by sunlight.

The boteco was on a block with a few other shops, all of them closed, almost no signs of life. "Espera," I told the driver. He nodded; waiting meant driving me home as well, doubling the fare. It was the early afternoon, and some men sat out front, drinking beer. They sensed my strangeness at once. It was my sex, my class, my foreignness. Everything was visible on the surface. I didn't look at the men drinking but went to the counter, a man in a white apron.

My husband lost his phone, I said in halting Portuguese. And I believe the phone is here.

The man stared at me without answering. I am looking for the phone of my husband, I said.

There was a rack behind the counter where I could see cigarettes and packs of gum. He poked around, and came back with a new SIM card. He was offering to sell it to me; he thought this was what I wanted. No, I said. The phone of my husband. Do you have some phones? The phones of other people?

I knew the men outside, the men drinking, had stopped talking in order to watch what was happening, wondering what this strange foreign woman was looking for in a place like this.

Maybe you have the phone there, I said, pointing toward a door at the back. The man turned and looked at the door, and then he turned back to me and shook his head. I glanced outside. The taxi driver was smoking a cigarette and chatting with the men. He looked perfectly at ease with them. I knew they were asking about me, what on earth was I doing.

I was becoming increasingly distressed. One of the men outside came in; he wanted to check on me. Senhora, can I help? What do you need?

"Tudo bom?" the taxi driver said when I finally went back outside. "Voltar?" He was asking if I wanted to go home. I looked around at the men, the beers in their hands, all of them silent now, watching me with the stupid, unconcealed stare people use for celebrities. "Sim," I said. I realized I was on the verge of tears.

Later, I thought of telling my husband what I had done, but, imagining what he would say, I decided against it.

I thought about the boys who robbed us. I had an idea of their lives. A culture of violence, alien and extreme; a world of dark streets, arbitrary punishment and deprivation, gangs, armed children, a kind of steady viscerality. No one offered them help. If they were killed, the police wouldn't bother to find the killers. Everything around them advertised the low price of their lives. They were ragged, malnourished, they were not physically imposing young men. Even the weapon they used to rob us was cheap and makeshift—there was tape on the handle of the knife. Society didn't protect them, and so they had no incentive to obey the boundaries society created to protect others. For them, abandonment and freedom were inseparable; by freedom, I mean the freedom they felt to violate the rules others followed. The consequences of being caught robbing us were not significantly worse than the consequences of not robbing us. If they had begged peacefully, if they had asked for charity, we wouldn't have given them anything.

Unemployment, if nothing else, gives you time to think.

For instance, it is insane to walk down a city street in America and expect the homeless men there *not* to attack you and rob you.

I wondered if that boy had ever used his knife on a woman whose purse he wanted. It was an enormous blade, more enormous now in memory. The fact that he had taped up the handle only made the threat seem more authentic. I felt a horizon of rage expand within me, long and bright, something like what I imagined my husband was feeling when he spoke of killing the boy who had the knife. The rage was simple, satisfying, and I savored the sensation as it melted out of me like ice.

I couldn't think of the boys as thieves. Jean Genet was a thief.

Thief—from Old Saxon and Middle Dutch, and a whole gene pool of other dead tongues. I find it difficult to come across a word and not think about its origins. This ends up being debilitating, as you might imagine.

FALSE COGNATES

I was out wandering in the neighborhood, waiting for my husband to come home from work, when I was caught in a sudden rain. It was evening. I went into the nearest store, a bookshop; the shelves of blond wood and ordered rows of spines seemed to collect and cast back the warmth of the shop's lamps. I walked through, in no hurry. There was a café, the fragrance of espresso. I felt better. I was in fiction, then nonfiction, then something else. There was a case of English-language books, out of order and seemingly chosen at random. I liked the inconsiderate chaos of it. I used to be depressed by the thought that you would never read every book that was worth reading—you wouldn't be able to read even a significant percentage, and much of what you did read would turn out to be dull or unoriginal or simply forgettable. In this light, any bookshop came to seem almost pointless in its abundance; its infinity of print mocked a lifetime's finiteness. My friend Helen, when I told her this, said she didn't understand me at all; and later I came to think she was right, that I was worrying about the wrong things. I found a shelf of novels by Clarice Lispector. I'd read something of hers once, in an English translation; harrowing. She was a diplomat's wife. She and her husband had lived in Naples, Washington, Switzerland. In letters she complained of the cocktail parties. I pulled down one of her books and flipped at random to an interior page. "É como se eu tivesse uma moeda e não soubesse em que país ela vale." Money is confusing, in other words. Then I went back to the beginning and in my mind's English read the first sentences: "– – – – – – am searching, I'm searching. I'm trying to understand."

I knew other Americans in São Paulo. My husband had some American co-workers, and he knew Americans working at the other banks. Americans sometimes turned up. I overheard English at the cafés on Rua Oscar Freire.

There was a little collective, which privately I referred to as the Wives. We formed a circle because of the language we spoke, the roles we inhabited. We gathered together over time as if by some natural process; every other week I met someone new, and someone else stopped coming. I was once the new person. There were lunches, afternoon drinks; we ordered bottles, sauvignon blanc. I knew diplomats' wives, the wives of company lawyers. The Mormon wives didn't drink, but they laughed and gossiped as much as the drinking wives. The women who had children had nannies as well.

I met the Wives at a restaurant that was all windows, no walls; it was a shrine of glass and status anxiety. The point of all that glass was to look. The lunchgoers looked at one another, the passersby on the street looked in at the lunchgoers, and the lunchgoers occasionally looked out to see who was looking in. All that looking was highly contagious. You looked at strangers with more interest than you looked at your companions. It was a palace, a temple of looking.

The Wives had lived in London, Miami, Budapest, Nairobi, Hyderabad, Kuala Lumpur, they had lived all over, moving always because of their husbands' jobs. They spoke about the boredom of interesting places. We were all of us ancillary. Expatriates had a way of talking selectively about the past. It was a perk of the lifestyle; no one asked for the full story. They talked about the way things were done in other countries, how the roads were, the horror of traffic, what you could buy in the grocery stores.

Karen said that when she learned she and her husband were moving to Brazil, she cried for three days. "But now I love it here. My husband found this bar in Pinheiros, we go and listen to music. You would love it. Brazilian music." Rachel said, "My greatest fear isn't growing old. It's going blind. They've done the laser eye surgery twice already, and it keeps wearing off." Whitney said, "Every time I come here, the prices have gone up." Alexis mentioned Stanford, a degree in history. "So you and I are roughly equals in unemployability," she said, addressing me. Vanessa said, "My mother had a great-uncle who lived in Brazil for years, up in the central savanna. He was a rancher, raising cattle. I can't even imagine." Lucy said, "There were no wild years for me." Karen said, "God, I hate São Paulo sometimes." Whitney said, "Do yours talk about old girlfriends in a way that tells you they still keep in touch?"

Stephanie had lived for a time in Addis Ababa. She talked about the absence of modern technology; her style of complaining was to make a show of not complaining. "I almost never read e-mail, there was no Wi-Fi anywhere. Life without all that was such a revelation," she said. "I did all this thinking that's impossible to do anywhere else. Ethiopia is such a spiritual place."

I went out of the restaurant into bright, post-wine afternoon light. I walked with Alexis and Rachel toward Avenida Paulista. Something was happening there. Traffic was stopped. It was a demonstration of some kind, maybe a few hundred people. Some carried signs. It wasn't immediately clear what was at stake. I heard chanting, whistles. Rachel asked what it was. "Oh," Alexis said, "labor grievances or something. They're like the French here. They're always on strike."

Marcos, my husband's co-worker, had the idea that I should give English lessons, and offered himself up as my first client. I didn't hear this directly from him; my husband acted as intermediary. "Marcos already speaks English," I said. My husband responded by pointing out that I would have to be paid in cash. It happened suddenly: I was a tutor of English. A tutor, not a teacher—teachers have relevant degrees.

I streamed some videos whose intended audience was people learning English as a foreign language. I thought that if I saw things from the student's perspective I would make a better tutor. This led me to a video in which a Finnish teenager "speaks" different languages—that is, she babbles nonsensically while replicating the music and cadence of more than a dozen tongues. She conveys amusement, boredom, anger, sarcasm, and exhaustion without ever using actual words, always convincingly, even in "English." This all looked like a lot more fun than actually learning a new language.

My single qualification as a tutor was the ability to speak a language whose deep grammar I had acquired before I could independently use the toilet. But apparently Brazilians did this, they hired stray Americans as language tutors; the market proved that people would pay money for instruction from someone with no training. I assumed I was less expensive than someone with training. Michelle, one of the Wives, said she knew several American women who had picked up tutoring work this way. So it seemed these Brazilians never stopped to wonder if they could turn around and teach a foreigner Portuguese.

At our first lesson Marcos told me he was looking for "refinements." He spoke as if I were a shopkeeper and refinements were a kind of tiny, hard-to-find screw he needed to fix his watch. The fact that he knew the word *refinements* suggested there was little I could do for him. I asked what the Portuguese was for *refinements*, and the word he used translated more literally to "perfectings." Already, the lesson was facing the wrong way.

Late at night, prostitutes waited for men in cars to stop and roll down their windows. This would happen a few blocks from our apartment. The prostitutes were tall, with tight skirts, strong shoulders, long, smooth hair. They used to be men. One lived in her car; I often saw her in the daytime on the sidewalks, shouting at people. Once, as I walked past, she spoke to me. I'm sick, she said.

My husband sat in an armchair, reading. I was in theory reading as well, but I couldn't concentrate, and kept looking at him. Of course, I'd spent much of the day reading already. My husband's face made an expression of trying to shut out the world in order to focus on the words in front of him. I turned to a new page in my book, and he swiped to a new page in his. He sat with good posture. He had good genes. He exercised. I asked him to read aloud something from his book. "'When the British tried to levy a hut tax—a tax of five shillings to be raised from every house—in January 1898, the chiefs rose up in a civil war that became known as the Hut Tax Rebellion,'" he said. It was a work of economic history that purported to explain the inequality among nations. I said: "Is it considered a civil war if they were rebelling against their colonizers?"

I performed virtually all the housework—it almost goes without saying. My husband didn't ask it of me, and he made a nominal effort, but he was at work all day and I was at home all day, so. I had no instinct for it, no homemaker gene, which, whether you want to admit it or not, some women do in fact possess. Some women do not feel especially put upon to find themselves washing a husband's underwear; I felt put upon. But I also felt the anxiety of the non-earner, of household dead weight, and so I washed my husband's underwear without mentioning to him, or to anyone, how strange it made me feel. Perhaps this was the start of resentment; but to resent my husband, I would have had to believe he'd stolen me away from a career, a path I wanted, and of course that wasn't the case at all. If it weren't for my husband, I would have been in New York authoring a fresh tweet about an exciting new blended cement—blending your cement guards against bleeding and inhibits sulfate attack—made from supplementary cementitious materials such as fly ash, hydrated lime, and furnace slag.

In New York, I was spared, because of my husband and his job. I was spared a certain kind of apartment in a certain kind of marginal neighborhood, roommates scavenged from the Internet, furniture scavenged from the street—a shipwreck life. I knew those things, I had done those things; but not for as long as I should have. Splitting a two-bedroom apartment four ways, foldouts in the living room, and always avoiding the landlord. I knew people who lived like that. The people who lived like that told me about it over coffee, over drinks, my treat. I had friends who spent their waking hours in cafés, working on their novels, screenplays, art concepts, graphic designs. They inhabited colonies of people like themselves, all hunched forward slightly in front of laptop screens, seated in rows behind their shields of glowing apples. They gentrified. I should have been made to suffer more. I should have had to live with the moral knot of gentrification, of being one of the gentrifiers. Instead I had a view of the Hudson from an apartment in Tribeca that a real-estate agent had found. I should have been deprived, because of who I was and what I wanted, what I did not want, what I enjoyed; because of what I could and could not do. Could: write a coherent sentence, handle a first-declension Latin noun (e.g., *latebricola*, *latebricolae*—"one who lives in hiding"). Could not: conduct a regression analysis, code in Java or Python, handle tools, afford health insurance.

Marcos's wife, Iara, made an effort to look after me. She once spent five months in San Diego studying English and had nothing but good things to say about America. She was a housewife, a mother, but the childcare they paid for seemed to take the sting out of motherhood; she was free during the days. One afternoon she took me to an exhibition of photographs at a gallery in Vila Madalena. The photographer was French. His subject was crowds—faces, bodies, community, anger. They were photographs of demonstrations and had simple titles: *Beirut*, *Islamabad*, *Istanbul*, *Gaza*, *Sanaa*. There were no dates. The titles of two photographs could have been switched without anyone knowing. It was impossible to distinguish the wailing women and rock-throwing men of one place from those of another.

The photographer's trademark was close-up shots of groups. In his pictures you saw only faces, no surroundings. People filled the frame like paving stones. And they were gorgeous images. The photographer aestheticized rage and suffering. I supposed they didn't resent the photographer's presence: wailing and rock-throwing are acts of performance; demonstrators want to be photographed. The pictures felt familiar, the way every morning the newspaper feels familiar. You came away with the sense that political despair was a universal and permanent condition.

"This one looks a bit like you," Iara said. Her finger hovered over the face of a woman near the front of a crowd. She had dark hair and skin, brown eyes, and was perhaps my age but in almost every other way was different from me. "I know she doesn't look exactly like you," Iara said, anticipating my objection, "but the shape of her face, the way her chin is like this, it reminds me of you. She is like the Palestinian protestor version of you."

John Singer Sargent's *Madame X*, which hangs in the Metropolitan Museum of Art, always reminded me of my mother—of my mother not as I knew her from memory, but as I knew her from pictures taken in her youth. It hadn't occurred to me previously that if Madame X (who in truth was a socialite named Virginie Amélie Avegno Gautreau, and whom Sargent painted when she was twenty-five years old, about the age I would have been when I first saw her portrait) resembled a previous edition of my mother, then she must, in some way, resemble me. I don't believe in past lives. But for a long time I used to have the feeling that someone, somewhere, had already done whatever I was going to do.

Iara was looking at a photograph of a suffering child. "Just because it makes you feel something doesn't mean it is art," she said.

In our building there lived a boy of no more than nine or ten who wore the uniform of what I knew to be an excellent and expensive private school. He spoke eerily fluent English. He was like a little American boy. He asked questions when I saw him in the elevator. Sometimes I felt as if I were being interviewed. He had the glossy brown hair of a boy in a T.V. ad, the kind of large brown eyes that seduce parents into recklessness.

Marcos had recommended me highly, the man said. I had the impression that Marcos had said something else to him, that I was a kind of charity. "The American wife has time on her hands," etc. The man's office had quite a view: a deep, cinematic plunge into the heart of the city. Helicopters sailed along the axes of the skyline, floating at the limit of my eyesight, like ships on a horizon. A good number of high-rise apartment buildings in this part of the city had mansard roofs or other architectural elements from the past—the idea being to make those buildings look older than they really were.

Some people had a sincere desire to improve their English for professional reasons, or they had an intellectual love of language; for others, I came to understand, keeping an English teacher on the payroll was proof of status. And I came to see that my skills as a tutor weren't the thing that mattered, only whether or not I was liked.

Obediently I began to think of these people as my clients. The client I liked best was an obstetrician who worked at the city's most exclusive hospital. Her name was Claudia. Claudia was in her forties, and she had a directness of manner and speech that impressed me, a sense of her bearings; the way she carried herself made me think male colleagues would know better than to mishandle her. At the hospital she attended several foreign women per month and wanted to communicate more easily with them. The husbands are always more nervous than the wives, she said.

"And I always know when one of them, one of the husbands, is not faithful," she said. I gave lessons at her apartment in the evening or, occasionally, the early morning. When we met in the morning her family would smash around through breakfast in the next room. They were people I heard and never saw. "He will give a lot of time talking to the male doctors and talk with me not so much. Only the husbands who are guilty cannot talk to an attractive woman," Claudia said.

"He will *spend* a lot of time," I said.

To prepare for our lessons, I taught myself medical vocabulary. The terms were unfamiliar to me even in English—*vernix*, *lochia*, *oedema*, words that weren't English, really, but specimens cut from the cadavers of Greek and Latin and then preserved in the formaldehyde of a medical dictionary.

I worked for Claudia; I was her employee. She had other employees. This was a category of people in her life, the category I belonged to. I saw the housekeeper when I came to the apartment. Days for Claudia's housekeeper began very early and ended very late. She arrived in darkness and left in darkness. I was paid more by the hour but was involved much less intimately in Claudia's life than the housekeeper, a woman who bought groceries and changed the linens and walked the two dogs and polished the frames of the family photographs; and yet I was the one who came by way of the social elevator, like a guest. Claudia never required me to use the service elevator—which the housekeeper surely never had to be told that she was expected to use. The difference, I supposed, was that I also lived in an apartment like Claudia's. She was indeed an attractive woman.

Marcos paid me in envelopes. Claudia folded bills around her thumb and then handed them to me. In one case the money was invisible, in the other it was unregarded.

It was work whose purpose was to relieve boredom rather than to earn a living—which made it not work at all, but a pastime.

Sometimes my husband met me after work for a drink at a boteco near Maison Monet. It was on the corner, by a frozen river of traffic, the chairs arranged carelessly on the sidewalk. The neighborhood men clustered there in the evenings, eating pastéis and bolinhos, while the owner himself brought out more bottles of Antarctica beer. Some nights musicians would set up inside and play songs of old Brazil. The men at the tables talked and talked. It was a country of never-ending social obligation, social approach. We knew the owner—the bar had been his father's, it had been in business fifty years. Passengers in cars stuck in traffic would roll down the windows and chat with the men at the tables, and one of the men would hand over a glass, a sip of cold beer before the light changed, a fleeting scene under the city glow of dusk. Evenings: the ashtrays quickly filled up, and the owner came around to replace them.

"Although usually you come home much later than this."

"I wouldn't say usually."

"You're frequently absent."

"I don't think that's fair."

"Let me say it differently, then. This is nice, being here with you like this. I wish it happened more often."

"The reason I stay late isn't that I don't want to be here."

"But you like what the late hours signify. You're central to the enterprise. Without you, the ship would sail off course."

"I want to be good at my job, yes."

"My point is that you already miss things."

"I wouldn't miss anything important. Not something truly important."

Brazilians loved to tell you about New York City. They had been there, they hadn't been there, and in any case they had glowing reviews. Here I am referring to rich Brazilians. Everything is so organized, they said. Everything works so well there, they said. They would all live there if they could.

After a lesson at his office, Marcos gave me a ride. It wasn't the direction he would go normally, but he had a dinner in Brooklin; my husband was at a dinner as well, somewhere else. "Blindado," I said, touching the leather detailing on the inside of the door. Bulletproof. I'd learned the word from the signs hanging at every car dealership—bulletproofing your vehicle was the standard practice. But Marcos corrected me: his car was unproofed. "If you have it, they notice you. It is not a good idea unless you are already a target. I don't want to be asking for attention. People here have cars that are much more…" He didn't have the word he wanted in English. I supplied it: "Flashy." "Flashy," he said, taking possession of the term. "Yes. This is what I want to avoid."

I learned that the name of my neighborhood came from the Tupi-Guarani word for *lie*. Apparently, there was an epic poem written in the late eighteenth century—which, I was assured, all Brazilians once knew by heart—in which the word was used as the name of a female character. She was symbolic, the incarnation of false love.

My husband invited me to join him at an airline-industry trade fair. It was part of an annual convention. I'd never been to a convention of any kind and was curious. For centuries *conventional* pertained simply to any agreement between parties, to coming together, and only in later usage did it swerve into synonymy with *unoriginal*, and then *boring*. He said there would be cocktails.

The booths were like little stages: elevated, illuminated, gleaming with expensive chrome surfaces. Those booths cost money—you have to buy to sell. There were booths for tarmac guys, engine-part guys, emergency lighting system guys. I admired a booth that belonged to a designer of cabin interiors. A quartet of airplane seats was on display to show off the company's work. The lighting was soft and invitational. Everything about it was the opposite of actually being on an airplane. Passing conventiongoers stopped to regard the seats as if they were art.

He hadn't lied about the cocktails. At many of the booths, women dressed like private escorts mixed caipirinhas and chatted with the men who approached. Men wandered the convention floor solo, with the verve of partygoers. The women moved in groups and seemed less sure of themselves.

From the far end of the hall, I heard shouting—a sound growing, something happening, but I couldn't see what it was. My husband was elsewhere. I went in the direction of the noise and arrived in time to see a group of men in matching blue jackets celebrating. They gave the impression of a tribe. People nearby smiled, the way spectators smile at a winner in a casino. I had no idea. I was the anthropologist, missing information. There were drinks at a nearby booth, and I went there. A girl gave me a caipirinha and a man who was standing nearby spoke to me in Portuguese. I smiled, out of instinct, which must have encouraged him; he kept going even as I failed to understand almost anything he said. His face was tanned, shining. I detected a kind of spoiled masculinity in him, a negative current in whatever he was saying. He talked ceaselessly, as if he would lose me the second he paused for breath. I knew that at any moment he would begin to touch me. I moved away. He never stopped talking, and I never stopped smiling.

"Why are we here? Why are you here?"

"You know. Meeting people."

"To what end?"

"You never know who you're going to meet."

"Networking."

"Networking."

"You're fishing for clients. Investment opportunities."

"I'm interested in certain indicators about the future of Brazilian aviation that will drive specific portfolio decisions."

"So you're spying."

"*Spying* is a pretty melodramatic word for what I'm doing. I'm listening. I'm collecting information. I'm not being secretive about it—I'm giving out business cards. I'm here to read signs. I get paid to predict the future. You're making fun of me."

"There's a sign," I said.

The sign said: COMO MONETIZAR SUAS RELAÇÕES. I wanted to ask them about it—I would have liked to know how to monetize my relationships. At the booth were two women, wearing absurd dresses and holding pamphlets. I owned shirts that were longer than the dresses those women wore. They looked like women who knew how to monetize relationships.

I said this to my husband and he laughed. He also did an admirable job of restraining himself from staring at the women's legs.

Respectable Brazilian newspapers published reports on actresses who had recently disrobed on camera. The actresses gave interviews about it, about what it was like to be naked, about the regimes of fitness and diet they used to prepare. The newspapers faithfully debunked rumors of body doubles, because it would have been tragic to learn that the actress who was naked on screen wasn't the same actress who was giving an interview about it.

De: a privative. Some knowledge is more monetizable than other knowledge.

Brazilians bought more plastic surgery than anyone else in the world. There was an epidemic of fake tits, and among men the vogue was calf implants, apparently. Women danced in the Carnaval parades naked, or as good as naked—they wanted their pictures in the newspapers. This was considered completely normal behavior. In my life, I had seen so many pairs of other women's breasts on television and in movies; a naked pair of breasts was now as common a sight as an old man waiting at a bus stop. Manet's *Luncheon on the Grass* provided the template for society—men wearing suits, women wearing nothing. There was now the presumption of female nudity. You could tell a man was disappointed when a television show didn't have some breasts, as if this were a breach of contract.

At Claudia's: "I have to go mother. *Mother*—I may use it as a verb also, yes?"

Her daughter had forgotten something. Claudia needed to go out and rescue her child from the absence of whatever it was she forgot. I was instructed to wait for her return. I was thirsty, and felt that Claudia would want me to help myself to a glass of water. I drank the water. Then I walked down the hallway. It did not seem like something I would ordinarily do, prowling. I heard noise coming from one of the rooms.

It was Claudia's teenage son, sitting in front of a computer screen. I saw the jagged fumbling of video footage, heard a subverbal human sound, before he realized I was behind him and closed the browser's window. I assumed he'd been watching pornography. He didn't seem embarrassed. He said nothing and after a moment opened the browser again. "You can watch if you want," he said.

A crowd surged, seethed. I saw the anger in people's faces. They carried signs, the writing in Arabic. The presence of police in military gear and the low quality of the video generated the expectation of violence. "You want to find the cell phone videos to know what it was really like," Claudia's son said. He spoke good English, better than his mother's. I went toward him, the screen.

I asked if what we were seeing was Egypt. "No," he said, "Tunisia. Egypt is next."

We watched videos. They had no beginnings and no ends, broken shards of protest activity. Everything happened in medias res. In one video, somebody collided with the man holding the camera—the cell phone—and it fell, and for the next ten seconds we watched the shuffling of feet, oddly peaceful, like a herd of cattle in a pen. The video suggested a way of contemplating an event: to shear it totally of context; to divorce it from narrative; to isolate it like bacteria on a slide. There was only this moment of failing, swimming focus, both calm and delirious, somehow authoritative. The caption gave the place and date, nothing else: "Cairo, 28 January." The person who made the video and uploaded it to the Internet had fished out a single moment from the stream of time, a moment that now had no way back to the stream from which it came.

Claudia's son's name was Luciano. He had attended an expensive private school, a school with a reputation, and now he was supposed to be studying for the university entrance exams. He was enrolled in a preparatory class, the cursinho. The exams meant everything in Brazil among a certain caste; he had failed once already. I knew, from what Claudia told me during our lessons, that Luciano's interests in life were inchoate. She spoke as a mother, concerned. Claudia said she did not know his friends, and only a couple of years ago he didn't behave like this. Something had changed for him. He was seventeen. I asked what signs she was seeing, what troubled her. "The books he is reading are not the books he has to read for his exams," Claudia said.

The boy I found wasn't reading books at all; he was watching videos of revolutions on the other side of the world. Luciano's hair was long, falling in rich black curls, he had dark hands. "So this is what interests you," I said. He didn't respond. I left him with his videos, the multiple chat windows he had open; he typed without looking at his fingers. I wasn't alarmed. I had the sense that he was a boy, doing boy things, poking around in weird holes. Claudia was a mother. Mothers worry. An interest in videos of the Arab Spring made sense to me—a seventeen-year-old wants to see evidence of people in the world whose actions have consequences beyond a score on an exam, a status update, whose lives are not bound by the same set of rules. The bedroom smelled humidly of boy, boyhood, a sweetish smell of skin on which sweat had formed and dried and formed again, as though he hadn't gone out in days.

Notwithstanding my new job as an English tutor, I continued my own study of Portuguese. During our lessons Fabiana would deplore the state of Brazilian politics. It was clear to me that her disdain for the ruling party was the result of love that had soured. She was a passionate woman. She had fierce attachments to individual politicians. She wanted to love them, and when love failed, she had nowhere to turn but hate. Politics mixed with the finer points of language. She could veer from the Workers' Party to the problem of false cognates in a single sentence. "Fui decepcionada," she would say, meaning not that she had been deceived, but that she had been disappointed, as only a lover can be. She was fond of the language teacher's old warning about "false friends," an injunction I remembered from as far back as sixth-grade French. I faithfully corrected my own clients when they said they were pretending to buy birthday gifts for their wives.

"Anyway."

"Anyway, what I'm hearing—you wouldn't believe it. The money. Where it comes from, where it's going. And everyone knows. It's a way of life here. After a while you assume the worst."

"Your bank is part of this?"

"No, I'm talking about the internal practices of other companies, their relationships with government. Governments, plural. What we do is watch what happens. Understand the lay of the land. It's routine surveillance."

"So you aren't personally implicated."

"Don't talk about this when Marcos is around, by the way," he said.

"Not that any of this would be news to him."

Iara arrived at the restaurant with tears in her eyes. I thought perhaps she had been arguing with Marcos and was trying to wipe away the evidence. But this wasn't the case; Marcos had water in his eyes as well. They said there was a protest. They said the police had used tear gas while they were trying to cross the avenue where the protestors were marching. They said they saw a police officer swing at a young man with his truncheon. The restaurant served Lebanese food. The air was warm, an aroma of coriander and mint. The table linens were paisley. They went to the bathroom to wash the gas out of their eyes.

"What were they protesting?"

"An increase in the bus fare."

"Was it a large increase?"

"Twenty centavos."

"They were protesting twenty centavos?"

The avenue where the protestors were marching was named in memory of a revolt in São Paulo in 1932, against President Getúlio Vargas, who ruled without a constitution. The revolt came after popular demonstrations across the state and the killing of four student protestors; there was another avenue named in memory of the four students. A couple of decades later, Vargas, then serving a different term of office and facing a different political crisis, committed suicide in the palace bedroom in Rio de Janeiro, in his pajamas, on the day of Saint Bartholomew's feast.

I felt pain. I tried to ignore it for a day, and then another, without admitting to myself that I knew what it was. Then it became too much, and I took a taxi to the hospital.

I had never been inside a hospital that didn't feel like a precinct of illness, that made you forget what it was there for, but this one almost succeeded. It had many floors and many wings, like an ocean liner. It offered valet parking. At last I found the elevators—eight elevators arranged in a ring, like men standing in judgment. I was bewildered to discover they had no call buttons. A docent, seeing my confusion, ushered me to a central console, where after some discussion he entered the number of the floor I wanted; the console's screen then told us which of the elevators would take me there; and then the button-pushing was over, as I needed only to stand in the elevator while it went automatically to my floor. It was a specific kind of inconvenient convenience: a system that seemed futuristic because, in addition to requiring a more complex internal computer, it redistributed the normal labor of elevator use—pushing buttons, choosing floors—in a novel way without eliminating any of it. The docent who loitered near the elevators was necessary to translate all that modern efficiency to the laity. It was as if the advancing edge of technology had returned us to a time when a little man sat in the elevator box and worked the controls for you. For some reason the hospital was named after Albert Einstein.

The intake at internal medicine was like the intake in heaven. Everyone wore white, the counters were white, the light was white. Even the silence of the room seemed white, bleached of agony: a hush lay over the people gathered there. I waited for my number to be called. Some people spoke English, some seemed to understand my Portuguese, some didn't. I missed things. Other people missed things. I went unnoticed, and then I was fussed over. It was dreamlike, or like being drunk, navigating unfamiliar space in a haze of language confusion, of things half-said, half-heard. The woman at intake asked questions I only partly understood and typed things into a computer as I talked, or didn't talk. It wasn't possible to describe the pain of a bladder infection without resorting to the metaphor of burning; but metaphors were a luxury in this situation. I said as little as I could, and hoped to be allowed to see a doctor. Silence seemed less risky than speech. Better to say nothing than to say the wrong thing. Soon I became afraid even to nod: to consent, in a medical situation, to something I didn't comprehend.

Claudia could have helped me. It was the hospital where she worked. But I hoped not to see Claudia there. I wanted her to think of me as a tutor, not a patient. It would only have confused things for each of us to become a client in the other's eyes.

Finally I was able to see a doctor. His name was Neuenschwander. When he asked in Portuguese what the problem was, I realized I had none of the words I needed. I said there was pain. I used my hands in place of words. I said there was fire inside me. The doctor rubbed his jaw. We muddled on. I stopped making an effort to conjugate verbs; and so when I was describing the past, I could have been describing the present as well, the future.

The doctor went for it in English. It was decent of him; I smiled and let the whole thing be comedy. He asked about pregnancy—obviously, a pregnant woman wouldn't feel like herself. I told him I knew what I had; I knew my own body. He ordered tests.

After a long interval of waiting, the tests came back, and Neuenschwander received me again. He looked over the pages of readings, tapping each number with the side of his thumb and dipping his nose slightly each time, as if he were adding up a bill. Then he looked up at me and smiled. "Normalíssimo," he said. I had no infection. My body was giving me false warnings. That sounded like a good thing. But now he was concerned that something else must be wrong. He wanted more tests.

I didn't want more tests. I wanted to go home. Whatever was wrong with me wasn't what I thought was wrong with me. Maybe nothing was wrong with me. I felt certain that more tests would tell us nothing. Neuenschwander sought to soothe me into passive acceptance of his plan. Another doctor was brought in, and she looked over my results as well. They huddled. They appeared genuinely worried. I became worried. I tried to say that I didn't want any more tests. Perhaps this wasn't rational. I had never been wrong before about what was wrong inside me. Fear systematically invaded my mind: if the pain wasn't what I thought it was, then it might be anything. Apparently I could no longer read the signals my body was sending.

They insisted on transporting me in a wheelchair. This was ridiculous, but I couldn't say no. Being handled as if I were infirm made me feel infirm. There were two nurses, two people I hadn't seen before, driving me toward another exam room. Neuenschwander brought up the rear. I don't need a wheelchair, I wanted to say, except I had no idea how to say *wheelchair* in Portuguese, and anyway the decision didn't seem to be mine to make.

In the exam room, I realized that the test Neuenschwander had in mind was an intravaginal ultrasound. This is as unpleasant as you'd think. The two nurses prepped me. I didn't understand how people who wanted to help could seem so sinister. I was trapped in the momentum of hospital procedure. I was without my clothes. It was happening without my permission, without my knowing what was to come until it was already in progress. I couldn't stop it because I couldn't find the words, any words. I was by now in a state of very high emotion; and the emotion disabled my Portuguese entirely. I was divided between anger at what was being done to me and fear that they would discover something terribly wrong inside.

I was dressed. I'd regained some of my composure. I was in Neuenschwander's office for the third time. He was telling me that the tests were inconclusive. He said this as if they hadn't also been upsetting. It didn't mean that nothing was wrong with me. It meant that if something was wrong with me, they didn't know what. But maybe nothing was wrong with me. His language went around in circles. He was very cheerful about the whole thing. I still felt the pain, mildly. The pain of a bladder infection is bad enough—the pain of your own body criminalizing sex—without the possibility that the pain might not be what you think it is. I was at a loss.

My husband picked me up. He was surprised when I called and said I was at the hospital, and perhaps also faintly aghast. My husband didn't like hospitals—I suppose no one does—and to me he seemed uniquely reluctant to visit them; he once allowed an ear infection to render him nearly deaf before seeking treatment. In almost everything, he was a responsible person who managed the problems of life, but to go to a hospital for something he felt he should be able to handle himself offended his sensibility, a core of unarticulated ideas about self-reliance. When he arrived, though, he was the model of concern. He had come directly from work. His tie was askew: I found this detail somehow touching; he looked so much like a husband.

Eventually the pain left, in an inconclusive, unsatisfying way, ebbing out, like a tide. And *wheelchair* in Portuguese is nothing more than "chair of wheels."

The Wives—like a sorority, in the sense that you weren't allowed to choose your friends. Lunch was sometimes twice or even three times a week. I was often reluctant to go; and yet I became anxious if it seemed I had been left off an invitation. Any group, of course, once it grows large enough, begins to form subgroups.

My mother also suffered from bladder infections. She once told me so, and warned me that I might have the same problem. It was a rare instance of direct maternal counsel. She shook her head, almost imperceptibly, whenever a thought came to her that she did not want to share; she contained things. She didn't point out that the bad odds of genetic inheritance would obtain if I were ever to have a daughter of my own. That a woman's body is a kind of casino.

Helen wrote:

> Once, in college, you referred to the "petit bourgeois fascination with price." Somebody was back from Mexico and talking about how cheap everything was. Why do I still remember that? I recall, verbatim, the oddest things people have said to me. Specific things, of highly variable significance. I was complaining the other day

to my friend David about a woman we both know who uses emoji to excess, and David asked whether it's really so different from using a written system of hieroglyphics. "Nobody questions the seriousness of the ancient Egyptians," he said. Now I am forced to withhold judgment, which you know I hate.

It was late, and hot. From outside came the sound of a great splash: a large object falling into water. I looked up. "Somebody's in a pool," my husband said.

We met at a party, Manhattan, someone's apartment. The man who would become my husband wore a herringbone coat and dark jeans and was talking intently with a woman when I arrived. Later he came up to me, introduced himself, and offered to mix me a real drink; others couldn't trouble themselves beyond lazily stirring vodka into Sprite. He knew where the host kept the good liquor. I never learned who that woman was. I agreed to go on a date only with reluctance—finance guy. But he said Joan Didion, when I asked what he was reading, and later he told me a truly obscene dead baby joke. I knew the joke already, but it impressed me that he would risk that sort of thing with a woman he had just met.

Retrodiction refers to a prediction made about the past. It is a way to test a theory by applying it to known events, existing data sets, rather than events still to come. Einstein provided a famous example of this when his theory of general relativity accounted for the behavior of Mercury in a way Newton's physics could not. It is a useful method in a variety of fields, especially those seeking to predict events with long time horizons, fields in which you can't wait for the future. Instead, you imagine yourself into the past, prior to the last known occurrence—ice age, planetary alignment, evolutionary anomaly, financial collapse—and then see if your theory correctly anticipates a future that has already happened.

FINANCIAL CONSIDERATIONS

This happens earlier, in New York.

I live with another woman, Margo. Margo and I need a new sofa. The previous sofa became untenable following a bedbug scare, as well as too many evenings of carelessness while drinking red wine. Margo and I have agreed to split the cost of the new sofa.

I didn't know Margo before moving in with her. She put an ad on Craigslist seeking a roommate after her old roommate moved out of the city—financial considerations. Margo's requirements for a roommate made her a sensible match for me, and I convinced her that I was a sensible match for her. I had incentives for doing so—two bedrooms in Fort Greene, rent-stabilized.

During the bedbug episode, Margo packed all the clothes she owned into eight black forty-five-gallon trash bags and schlepped them to the laundromat, where she washed everything twice with hot water, using two full bottles of detergent.

Once the clothes were back inside the apartment, she became convinced that the remedy hadn't worked. Their eggs have ridiculous powers of survival, she said. The symptoms of having bedbugs are virtually identical to the symptoms of merely suspecting you have bedbugs. She said, Do you have any idea how much that cost? Then she started throwing away clothes.

Margo is in all important ways a fine roommate.

Ultimately, we had to hire an exterminator to assess the extent of the problem. He said he'd seen worse. Still, it cost money. I have a second credit card for these things, unforeseen expenses.

I explain the situation to the man who will become my husband. He says he's going to help. At first he thinks this means going with me to West Elm or IKEA. I laugh at him and start scrolling through advertisements for sofas on Craigslist. We've been dating less than a year.

He says, If I were the one who just survived a bedbug scare, I'm not sure how enthusiastic I'd be about buying a used couch.

I think to myself that this is a fair point.

After seventeen straight pages of sofa listings, my mind starts to wobble. People have no idea how to take photographs of their own furniture, and everything looks nauseating.

In the end, though, there are several plausible candidates, and we block off a Saturday for hunting. He suggests renting a van. I tell him that's unnecessary, and he asks if I plan to bring the sofa home on the subway. We go to the rental place, and he takes out his credit card, and I tell him of course not, and then I don't actually stop him from paying for the van. He also drives it.

The first used-sofa owner lives in Lefferts Gardens. She explains that she's moving to San Francisco for work and is selling all her furniture. This strikes me as a convincing non-bedbug explanation for why she no longer wants a perfectly good sofa. Her apartment has bay windows with a view of the park, and I'm tempted to ask her what the rent is, until she mentions offhand that her sister is taking over the lease. The sofa, unfortunately, is beige.

It looked different in the picture on Craigslist, I say to the man who will become my husband as we drive away.

I don't actually think of him as the man who will become my husband. If someone were to suggest to me that I should think of him that way, I would laugh, or gasp. I am sure I am in love with him, but I am also only twenty-three years old, and these two facts seem to stand in opposition. Love, in my mind, is a present-tense emotion, and has nothing to do with the future.

The next sofa, in Crown Heights, is perfect in every way except that someone beat us to it by twenty minutes and paid cash.

This happens two more times.

He suggests that we take a break for lunch. I say yes. The next used-sofa owner on my list isn't free for an hour.

You're worried, he says.

It's not going well, I say.

If we don't find one today, we'll try again next weekend, he says.

The van cost forty dollars.

That doesn't matter, he says.

I kiss him.

He asks, When is your lease up?

I'm subletting from Margo, I say. It's her name on the lease. But I suppose we have an understanding that I'll stay on when she renews.

When does that happen?

In two months.

Here's an idea, he says.

What?

Move in with me.

You live in Manhattan.

So.

I can't afford Manhattan.

Well, he says.

Absolutely not.

You sleep there four or five nights a week already, he says. We almost never sleep at your apartment. You work in Manhattan.

I can afford to *work* in Manhattan, I say.

The man who will become my husband smiles and eats the last of his cheeseburger.

I have three more sofas on my list. The first one we see after lunch looks exactly like it did online but has a faint smell. When the owner steps away for a moment, I ask, sotto voce, if he also notices it.

I wouldn't call that faint, he says.

When we're back in the van, he asks if I've thought about his suggestion.

That was less than an hour ago, I say.

You're worried about the rent, he says.

Do you have any idea how much I pay now?

No, he admits.

Seven-sixty a month.

We could find a new place, in Brooklyn.

You wouldn't move to Brooklyn.

At the next apartment, a cat greets us. Then another cat, and then another, and then another. When the owner finally appears, I see that her clothes are covered in cat hair. I tell her that we just bought a sofa and no longer need to see hers. She asks why I felt it necessary to tell her this in person. I apologize profusely for bothering her as we make our retreat.

I text Margo and tell her it's not going well. She would have come with us, but she has a deadline the next day and will forfeit ten percent if she's late on delivery to the client. I'm literally sitting on the floor right now, she replies. If I do what the client wants this site is going to give people epilepsy, she writes. If I don't do what the client wants the client won't pay me, she writes. Please find a couch!!!!, she writes.

I tell the man who will become my husband that we shouldn't even see the last sofa. It was the least appealing of the ones I put on my list, and at this rate I know something will be wrong with it.

We have the van for two more hours, he says. No reason not to.

He exudes reasonableness. He kisses me. We go and see the last sofa.

It's not bad. It's pale gray, firm, unstained. I text Margo, and she immediately replies with her approval. The owner knocks off fifty bucks because he's tired of exchanging e-mails with people about the sofa. He helps the man who will become my husband carry it downstairs to the van.

We all shake hands. The man asks where we live.

Fort Greene, I say.

I love Fort Greene, the man says. My wife used to live there.

But we might move to Manhattan, I say.

The man nods, takes this in.

No one I know lives in Manhattan anymore, he says.

That evening the three of us sit on the new sofa eating Thai food while Margo finishes the project for her client. She hands me ten twenty-dollar bills, her share of the cost, and I hand them to the man who will become my husband.

I'll pay what I owe you soon, I say to him.

No rush, he says.

BEAUTIFUL WORKS OF ART GUARANTEE A 100% EXPERIENCE

One night we returned to Maison Monet after another dinner in Jardins with another crowd of Brazilian financiers. Jardins was an old, exclusive neighborhood, and I had eaten a steak of poor quality in a room of gorgeous detail. My husband mentioned more than once how good his Chilean sea bass was. He and I were the only Americans at the dinner; the Brazilians were colleagues of his or clients—I lost track. They only wanted to trade rumors about the finance minister—would he be sacked, would he hang on, did he have any real power, who would replace him? Cardoso wasn't perfect, but at least he had ideas, someone said. My husband laughed knowingly. I didn't have enough information to laugh knowingly. As if any of it makes a difference, said one of the Brazilians. He gave a knowing smile. I was surrounded by knowing. The Brazilian winked so often, it seemed out of his control.

I once imagined that marriage would be the opposite of this—not that I wanted to constantly swap trivialities, but I anticipated a sense of union, consciousness not indistinguishable but in contact, contiguous. Two sovereign countries sharing an open border. I was twenty-five years old then and wanted *x*. Now I was at the edge of thirty and wanted *y*. By the time I turned thirty-five, I would want *z*.

My husband, a little drunk, said: "I was hoping for more." I asked what he meant. "More from them," he said. "They didn't talk about anything tonight." "Yeah, I had fun, too," I said.

When the taxi dropped us at our corner, a young woman in horn-rimmed glasses was there, absorbed in some kind of dance. She twirled, vibrated. She could have been a graphic designer or an office assistant, a perfect petit bourgeois type. She pounded her feet on the ground and turned in wild circles. The performance had a crude minimum of choreography, a desperate, sexual oiliness. She rubbed a liquor bottle all over her body as she danced—down her legs, between her breasts—and finally nuzzled it into her crotch. Her face had an expression of ecstatic anguish. She smashed the bottle on the ground and ran across the road to where a sedan with tinted windows was idling. Then the car drove off.

I asked my husband what we had witnessed. "Macumba," he said. "In macumba the crossroads are important, I think."

Macumba—witchcraft. At our gate he spoke with the porteiro, who had also seen the young woman; the man was having trouble controlling his laughter. I asked why he was so amused. "He said that ex-boyfriend is fucked," my husband said. So it was the dance of a jilted woman. It hadn't occurred to me previously that we were living at a crossroads.

Through a friend of Iara's I was put in contact with a priest who ran a refugee center at a church downtown. The father was taking in droves of Haitian refugees and he needed help. Here is a woman who speaks French and has time on her hands, the friend of Iara's said, or something like that.

The church was still considered a natural place of sanctuary. Anyone could go to a church. I was so far from all that, I sometimes forgot this was the case.

Droves of Haitians, and Syrians as well. You see the horrible news about what is happening in Syria, but when the Haitians come to us, they are in worse shape than the Syrians, the father told me. That's because the Syrians are fleeing war, but the Haitians are fleeing poverty. You can't escape being poor. When you are well-off, even if you lose all your money—you are still well-off, you know?

I liked Padre Piero at once. He had no English, and so we used Portuguese together; to communicate with the Haitians, Padre Piero spoke Italian with a French accent. In spite of circumstances, the father had a sense of humor. He was maybe forty years old. He wore glasses with stylish frames. I could imagine him walking through the streets of Rome in a suit.

He put me to work translating right away. A Haitian man calmly explained how he had come to Brazil. He left his small half island by boat, then went on foot through the jungle with an exorbitantly paid guide across the border from Colombia or Peru and into the territories of the Amazon, and finally traveled for days by bus. Others had come the same way. The bank had flown us to São Paulo from New York in business class. The route the Haitians used would have killed me. I didn't have to return to the church; but two days later I was back.

Droves—the term refers to cattle. You use it with people only when you don't feel like counting everybody.

When they discovered I was American all they wanted to know was whether I had connections in the American consulate. The Haitians used a sui generis mix of indecipherable English, fragmentary Portuguese, Creole French. They were thoughtlessly interested in acquiring U.S. visas, like lottery tickets—like nail scissors, something it's better to have with you than not. The men asked me about visas circumspectly, the women outright. Some of them talked about getting a visa the way you would talk about getting a gun—a thing that certain people obtained legally and certain people not so legally. Rumor and superstition came back to me in the form of insane questions that I couldn't answer. Is it true that the Americans prefer to see a statement from Banco do Brasil, that I should go early on a Tuesday morning, that I should mention a cousin in the United States and never a brother? Sometimes a crowd formed around Padre Piero, people holding out hands, papers. He would laugh and say, "Calma, calma." Newcomers were the most avid. In general, though, it was a zone of idleness, of waiting. Everyone learned how to wait. Everyone acclimated to tedium.

Life had been movement, danger, and uncertainty, and now life was waiting. The women on benches inside the church, the men standing around the dust of the church parking lot, everyone, men and women, reclining on floors. This was the reason they swarmed Padre Piero whenever he appeared—there was nothing else to do. Signs from an inkjet printer were posted around the church, or they were handwritten, bad French under the Portuguese—where the kitchen was, the bathroom, please don't sit here.

In a large hall, electric fans bolted high upon the walls. Men sprawled on mattresses Padre Piero himself had put down, hand luggage everywhere, blankets, shoes. A few of the men folded everything very neatly, but for the most part it was ramshackle, phones charging in every wall socket. A drugged languor, total inertia; only the fans stirred the air. Plastic bottles, half-full of liquids that didn't match the labels. Surely these men were bored out of their minds. For some reason the wall sockets were installed at eye level, and the phones, dangling by their cords, didn't reach the ground. I didn't see any books.

My main job was to help with papers. Haitians in Brazil were eligible for work permits and temporary residence. This was remarkable to me, an American accustomed to a diet of politicians vilifying immigrants. The Haitians spoke no Portuguese, and for some of them, any kind of writing was difficult; I didn't really speak Portuguese, and I didn't really speak Creole, but there I was.

The Haitians found work in construction, cleaning, factory jobs. Some worked on the metro. Prospective employers came to the church twice a week. "I need two," they would say. "I came for eight." Usually they were women, which surprised me, some of them older, women who owned carpet factories, small clothing businesses; they arrived with documents and went off with a couple of Haitians who had agreed to stitch blue jeans. "I have three already, I need three more," things like that.

For the Haitians, time was chalked off in periods of waiting. "Two more days." "They said four more days." They all knew the term *carteira assinada*. The carteira assinada was something official; and an official document was talismanic, stamped, signed, it would consecrate their existence. They traded numbers, the hoped-for salaries—one thousand, two thousand—rumors condensed to figures, amounts of money recited as if they were Hail Marys and Our Fathers.

They took turns using the limited number of available wall sockets to charge their phones. I would have expected a certain amount of resource conflict in all this, but it appeared to be a fairly relaxed economy, with a guiding principle of most in need, first in line.

The men were needy and occasionally impatient, but never impolite toward me, and never suggestive. I was used to the sensation, in public, of being visually appraised, the soft alarm of unwanted attention, especially near groups of men, but among these men I never caught anyone looking at me in a sexual way. I became newly alert to the racist things Brazilians said about Haitians living in their country, whom they often referred to as Africans.

Droves. It's one of those words; once the word comes into your mind, it becomes difficult to think of a substitute.

I saw the prostitute who lived in her car. She was pacing the block. She stepped in front of some young men and pulled up her shirt, exposing her breasts, enormous globes of artificial fat; the young men were laughing. She did it again, and in exchange one of the young men gave her a drink from the bottle of soda he was carrying, which must have been what she asked for. The young men walked on, still laughing, a small price to pay for entertainment. She was yelling at them as they left. I thought of a title: *The Power of Female Persuasion*.

Claudia was in a sour mood when I arrived. She was disappointed with her husband. He had started a business, she told me, an event-planning company, and it was failing; it never hadn't been failing. I asked what sorts of events he planned. Very few, she said. I told her to tell me about it, in English. I said it would be good practice. When I gave English lessons, it was the only time I didn't feel guilty for not speaking Portuguese with Brazilians.

From the start, Claudia said, she knew her husband's business was a terrible idea, but he believed it wasn't a terrible idea because he had start-up money. The money came from one of his brothers. Language instruction was intimate: you practiced language by talking about yourself. "I am an only child," Claudia said. "It saves me from doing stupid things. You make stupid decisions out of brothers and sisters." I was an only child, too, but for some reason I didn't mention this. "*Because* of brothers and sisters," I said.

I asked how her son was. Claudia made a face that said, Oh, children. Luciano worried her, she said, but so did her young daughter, highly emotional. "She is too much—what is the word—*dramatic*. She cares too much about *everything*." Did Luciano take an interest in his sister's well-being? "Luciano acts as if he does not have a sister. As if he does not have a *family*. Luciano, let me say, it is like he is the only person in the world."

My husband wanted a child. In his mind this was an unexceptional desire. He wanted a child, or, to be precise, multiple children, two or three, whereas the only number I was sure I was comfortable with was zero. He said that he had always wanted children, that he had always been honest with me about this, and of course that was true; he had always been honest. I didn't necessarily not want children. But the request made me feel like a vessel, a means to an end, and the world as I understood it made me doubtful about the ethics of having children, generally. I saw more reasons to be skeptical of procreation than reasons for enthusiasm. He found my logic vague. And so, over the course of months, a discussion about the possibility of a child had turned into an argument about the very idea of children, and that argument came to be a kind of molten core inside other conversations.

"You know, there is now a theory in psychology about mountains. It says that people who live with mountains around them are more quiet. More introspective. Because they are *surrounded*. People who live near the ocean talk more, they are more open to the world," a man said to me at a party.

We found evidence of black magic in our neighborhood. Empty champagne bottles on the sidewalks, cachaça bottles, burnt-down candles and dead roses, wooden crosses. During the night things appeared under the fiddlewoods and leopard trees, the jacarandas. These were the prayers of women: that the husband she secretly hated should die; that the man she loved who did not love her in return should become sick; that the wife of the man she loved should never conceive a child. Middle-class women did this. We went walking on Sunday mornings and saw these little dioramas of personal suffering. The macumba is the last resort of a woman who wishes for a reality that is different from the reality she knows.

I turned on the T.V. and found myself in the middle of a film. Vincent Cassel, the French actor with an interesting face, plays the role of an unhappy man involved in an affair. He is somewhere on the Brazilian coast. He broods; he speaks excellent Portuguese. In one scene, he wakes early while a woman sleeps by his side. This is the ultimate first-person moment: to be awake while someone else is sleeping. The implication in a film is that the sleeping person is innocent, unaware, or irresponsible, even insignificant, while the waking person is the opposite of these things: alert, burdened, morally complicated, profoundly conscious. When this happens in a film, and it's the woman who is awake, I sympathize; when it's the man, I lose it. On screen, Vincent Cassel stood, moved around, upset the silence of the room. There isn't a woman in the world who would have slept through that.

In Portuguese there is no unique word for *heaven*; the word is the same as the word for *sky*. I spent a lot of time watching the sky through the windows of the apartment. The skies of one place really are different from the skies of another. Half the cars in the city had bumper stickers that said JESUS CRISTO É O MEU SENHOR.

A man told me that notwithstanding being Brazilian he had an American passport, as if I needed reassurance of this, and that he owned an apartment in Orlando. We were in an elevator.

Noli me tangere. But he didn't say it in Latin, and the Latin isn't a good translation of what he did say, anyway.

When you live in a city, you know the landmarks but rarely visit. They are like prominent strangers and have the emptiness of strangers' lives. In the old center of São Paulo was a great, domed church presiding over a crumbling plaza lined with palm trees and frequented by drug addicts. Occasionally, a few tourists took photos or even went inside. I never did. But one day I noticed something. The crosswalk signals near the church weren't silhouettes of walking men, as they were elsewhere in the city, but rather little silhouettes of the church itself. This discovery delivered a burst of childlike joy. I found others. In Little Tokyo—Japanese lanterns. At the Museum of Art—a silhouette of the Museum of Art.

I saw a man in Centro with a sandwich board hanging from his shoulders. It said COMPRAMOS OURO, a phone number, the man's face without expression, his eyes not quite closed. The man held the sandwich board between thumbs and forefingers the way a different man would hold the lapels of his suit. Who has precious metals to sell and calls a number he sees on a stranger's chest? Then the answer came to me. This was where my husband's wedding band had gone, to a man who buys gold. The date of our wedding had been engraved on the inner curve—a sentimental touch, I know.

COMPRO OURO—*I Buy Gold.* COMPRAMOS OURO—*We Buy Gold.* COMPRA-SE OURO—*Gold Bought.* I saw the signs everywhere.

I was amused by the idea of my husband's investment bank advertising itself this way, my husband and the other men out on the street, in their Italian suits, sandwich boards hanging from their shoulders: WE BUY GOLD.

My husband called—still at work, nothing really, plans, the name of a restaurant. I read some reviews of the restaurant online. The reviews in Portuguese were riddled with colloquialisms, outside my ability to comprehend, and I used Google to translate, to see what I was missing.

> My relationship with this glass box has surpassed 16 years. His revolving door leads us to its central bar which is facing an uninhibited kitchen that allowed to watch the duty gluttons. Your unisex bathroom is an invitation to flirt rapid eye corner. Waiters and waitresses beautiful, sympathetic. His music is touching and not touching, yet sophisticated. Models, executives, fashionistas dictate the dress-code and behavior here. Go early or try to make a reservation because the auction of beautiful people, who do not mind waiting. The strong are meats. Sweet place to enjoy and celebrate the greedy, honest wine. The menu and wine list on iPad, enable appropriate harmonization. Price a bit steep, but nothing abusive. Beautiful works of art guarantee a 100% experience.

> I was with two other people and nobody answered us. Then the waiter made fun. We ordered three desserts and only one was served. We do not pay the service, since the service was lousy. The waiter who served us went to the door to make fun of our face again. And all this is a summary of many other embarrassing situations that I underwent. This has been a week.

> I went at night. The hall was empty. As I was not well dressed, no one came to meet me or take me to a table, so I walked in, sat down, and waited to be served. As I was alone, I jumped the entrance and went to the main course. I have made the request and asked for the waiter to repeat what he had written down. And guess what? My flesh came off. A simple dish should be better prepared.

"So when you find out about that sort of thing."

"We evaluate."

"You evaluate the decision to invest."

"In some cases we've already invested. We're evaluating the costs of pulling out our money, changing our position."

"So you *re*evaluate."

"Are you really curious about my work?"

"I'm curious about this particular thing."

"It's not a thing you talk about directly."

There was another protest, and then another. They were in São Paulo, in the cities of the south. News coverage grew. The police were reckless, cruel, people were injured. People who had not been protesting joined the protests in anger over what the police were doing. Other causes joined with the original grievance over the bus fare. Everything now had momentum.

Helen wrote:

> Don't you see? This is essentially an artist's residency. You're living in an unfamiliar city, you have tons of free time, a nice place to stay, there are drinks, and somebody else is paying the bills. Apparently there's even civil unrest. You should take advantage. All your starving vagabond experimental video artist friends currently being priced out of Bushwick would trade places with you in a second.

I wrote back:

> But I'm not an artist.

African slaves in Brazil practiced an improvised dance performance, called capoeira, in which two men appear to fight in slow motion. Their owners outlawed it. Slavery was abolished in Brazil in 1888, but capoeira remained illegal until 1937. The ban was lifted only when President Vargas—the same president the São Paulo rebels failed to remove from power in 1932 and who years later was found dead in his pajamas from a bullet through the heart—personally attended a performance and happened to like it.

There was an exhibition of art in an old maternity hospital. Iara brought me. The hospital was twenty years out of use; once upon a time half a million people were born there. Now it belonged to a French businessman who planned to turn it into a hybrid of shopping mall, luxury hotel, and "creativity center." I read as much as I could understand of an interview in Portuguese the French businessman gave to *Folha*. "Creativity can be sold," the businessman said.

Some of the artists were famous, some were young, and they all took to the idea of occupying a defunct hospital with the exuberance of children. The businessman called it a "creative invasion." Art stuff was everywhere, and it was not always obvious if something was new art or incidental hospital matériel. A stone bust of the hospital's founder might have predated the creative invasion or been an invention of one of the artists, designed to appear as though it predated the creative invasion. It could have been ancient or faux ancient. Debris commingled with the fruits of artists' labors; debris was the point. The walls of the hospital were crumbling, the paint was scaling, a dust of poisons hung suspended in air, asbestos and lead. The word for all this was *decrepit*. Wild plants grew everywhere, in sprouts and tangles; plant life climbed the exterior walls, jungly and lush. Once, the hospital would have seemed grand. Now it was an example of the decaying splendor for which there was an emerging market: ruin porn. Admission was free. But free doesn't exist. Free means only that someone else is paying, or that you're paying with something other than money. At the entrance was a backdrop emblazoned with the logos of banks, gas companies, investment firms, hotel chains, brands of vodka and champagne.

The exhibition was well-publicized. Not long after we arrived the line already extended around the block. Vendors sold water and fruit. The length of the line made it seem like part of the exhibition, performance art: a group of volunteers play-acting the role of people waiting in line for a popular exhibition. They behaved and dressed exactly as they would have behaved and dressed if an artist had conceived it.

If the exhibition hadn't been popular, the organizers could have paid people to stand in line and make it seem popular. I said this to Iara. "You can always pay somebody to do something," Iara said.

In spite of the crowd, some rooms were empty, even entire hallways. The old rooms and hallways, ghostly and unrestored, were more interesting to me than the art itself. Even the artists themselves seemed aware that the real attraction was the strange, low-grade thrill of visiting a place that ordinarily would have been off-limits. As if in acknowledgment of this, some of them simply signed their names to the walls of the dead hospital.

I asked Iara if she'd ever wanted to be an artist. She laughed. "I am not even a failed artist," she said. "But all your friends are artists," I said. "I like artists, I believe in art," she said. I hadn't thought of art as a matter of belief. "I think I only feel things about art," I said. "Yes, of course, you have to feel it," she said.

I saw a pair of destroyed foreign-made automobiles, one mounted on the other, like animals in heat. I saw bricks and other rubble gathered from broken floors and stacked into haphazard votive forms under the dirty light of old windows. I saw a sinister red glow beamed into a dark room frothing with machine-made mist. I saw the floor at the base of a marble stairwell transformed into a black mirror by half an inch of standing water. I saw doorways jammed full of magazines and newspapers and chunky 1980s-model desktop computer screens. There was a hospital chapel. Inside, I saw what you'd have to call lunatic party decorations, bulbous and hand sewn, hanging from the ceiling, brightening the altar, a fertility of color in the barren cave of religion. I saw exotic plants. I saw a maze of lights. I saw lumpy piles of white material, heaped onto a hospital bed, the shape of limbs, the size of bodies.

The article in *Folha* mentioned that a couple of well-known Brazilian artists had refused invitations to participate in the exhibition. The artists said they didn't want to be part of a publicity stunt to promote a real estate development. The businessman was unconcerned. He seemed to think he had plenty of creativity to sell with or without a couple of well-known Brazilian artists.

I saw something that seemed too obvious to be interesting as art. Painted on the whitewashed walls of an enormous room were the heads and bare torsos of seven young black and brown men. They were larger than life, much larger, floor to ceiling. Their faces showed varieties of feeling: a smile, a bashful downward gaze, a defiant stare, faces mournful, bemused, doubting, wry.

They were beautiful boys. I stared for a long time. They had gentle faces, gentle eyes. I was mesmerized, the way I became mesmerized in the presence of a Rothko or a Pollock. I was emotional. They were thin, bony, some had concave cheeks, flapping ears, black hair, thin mustaches. They were blazingly individual; because of their size they couldn't disappear into a group. Here were people typically not extended the courtesy of epic portraiture, was the point. Here were the young men of the favelas—when faces like theirs appeared in public, it was in newspapers or on T.V., in connection with poverty, crime, police violence; it wasn't like this. A kind of glow radiated from the wall, an effect of the lighting on the tones of the paint: to create the shades of the boys' skin the artist would have used red, russet, brown, ocher, beige, chocolate. There was no single word for the color of their skin. The other visitors at the exhibition looked like me, not like the boys, and this, too, was the point. The exhibition, the hospital itself—they were monuments to money. But these boys were monuments to themselves.

The faces loomed over me when I went to the corner of the room. Proximity and size transformed their expressions into something hard, aggressive. As a white woman I was conditioned to see any group of dark-skinned men as a threat. I waited. The humanity began to flow back into the faces, the range of feeling, the subtle individual electricity. The artist knew who would see his art; he had smuggled his subjects from zones of poverty into zones of wealth. I had been in the room with these boys for more than twenty minutes. That was the point—the attention you paid that you wouldn't have paid if you saw them on the street. The time you spent.

I heard an eruption of young voices. They were fifteen or so teenagers, black and brown kids. They went right up to the walls, the walls of the old hospital, to the colossal painted faces of the young men who looked like them. They touched the faces. Their behavior was not the behavior of regular art-goers. I saw a woman with them, someone my age; it was a field trip. The kids laughed. It was as if they had become part of the artwork, as if their response created an additional layer of meaning: young people who weren't usually the consumers of art looking at young people who weren't usually the subjects of art. And for them I might have been part of the artwork as well, the privileged white artgoer, an exemplar of the status quo, the kind of person who uses Latin terms in casual conversation. I had come to the exhibition and they were brought to the exhibition, by a white adult, a benefactor. I assumed they would not have come on their own. That day may have seemed exceptional in their minds; or perhaps I was inventing thoughts for them they didn't have. I doubted they noticed me at all, in fact. The quality of luxury is in the eye of the beholder.

Because it was always there, a bulge in the mind, the question of a child became itself a kind of pregnancy. When we weren't talking about it, I was aware that we weren't talking about it, and aware that he wanted to talk about it. Aside from my husband, there wasn't anyone I spoke of it with. For reasons I couldn't name I obeyed a marital omertà. I perhaps didn't want anyone to know that we disagreed about so fundamental a choice. And I thought perhaps I would be judged; wasn't my husband's preference the more normal? What sort of woman doesn't want a child?

The hospital was called Matarazzo, after its founder, an Italian who immigrated to Brazil and built an empire of plantations and factories, and who, in 1937, at the time of his death, was Brazil's wealthiest man. The hospital was one of his good works. Matarazzo's nephew later used the family money to found the São Paulo Museum of Art and the São Paulo International Biennial of Art. Now a wealthy Frenchman owned the hospital and intended to sell creativity, not to mention luxury hotel suites, and for the time being it was open to the public, who came in droves, and waited in lines, and delighted in the curiosity of touring an old building in decay, in the last days before it was torn down.

"Havia mais futuro no passado." The words were stenciled in Helvetica on one of the hospital walls. There was more future in the past.

THE CHILDREN'S PARTY

My husband accepted an invitation on our behalf to a children's party. It was the birthday of a co-worker's child. The party made me think of how children at Versailles must have celebrated their birthdays. It was the closest thing to a bacchanalia you could have involving nine-year-olds.

The venue was the Planet Kids Buffet Infantil: an elaborate multistory funhouse devoted to the pleasures of prehormonal children. These party zones were a minor industry, irrigated by money from the city's larger industries; all those bankers and plastic surgeons had kids. And seemingly every one of those kids received a fêting, annually, on a regal scale. The party zone supplied everything: activity leaders, photographers, videographers, courts for volleyball and basketball, stations where girls could have their nails painted and where boys could design papier-mâché swords, an indoor roller coaster, whole mountain ranges of balloons, three-layer cakes of chocolate and dulce de leche, actors dressed up as famous copyrights—fantasy characters that belonged to a time in childhood when the world seemed both sane and magical—and a full bar for the adults. The party zone handled theme requests: princess in a fairy tale; space adventure with superheroes; time travel with dinosaurs; cowboys and Indians in the desert. Evidently you were allowed to mix themes even at the expense of narrative continuity. The parents didn't have to do anything; they only had to swipe their debit cards. There was a cruise-ship atmosphere of outsourced responsibility. Everything was the color of candy. The kids were drunk on the overabundance of stimuli. The adults were drunk in the usual way.

And those kids—from the age of first memory, everything they could imagine was available to them. Often it was given to them without even being asked for. Catering was a fact of life.

They weren't growing up to be muggers; but they were growing up to be *something*.

It was a titanic crowd, and my husband quickly disappeared, possibly with the co-worker whose child was turning nine, but I couldn't be sure because no introductions were made. I found myself alone on the hostile terrain of Planet Kids. The only people I saw were strangers. I saw Spider-Man, Batman, the Incredible Hulk. I wasn't panicking, but I wasn't feeling well. Finally, I spotted João, and swam gratefully toward the oxygen of a familiar face.

"You are looking perfect," João said, kissing both my cheeks.

"I'm not the first woman you've said that to today," I said.

"But with them I was lying."

We talked about his work. João was a veterinarian. If men like to talk about something other than their work, they do an excellent job of hiding it. He was planning a new venture with a partner.

"Everything in one place. So we are not only taking care of the animals, but selling imported pet foods, equipment, things you cannot normally find in Brazil."

"There's a market," I said.

There were times when I talked like my husband in order to be understood.

"Let me show you," João said.

We went out to the street. João led me by the arm; I was grateful for the fresh air. He pointed at a woman being tugged along by two leashes attached to two small white dogs.

I said, "Do you know her?"

"I have no idea who she is. But how do I know she will be here? Because I see her everywhere. Everywhere you go in this city, you see women with dogs. I will tell you a fact. São Paulo is the city that has the greatest number of dogs under ten kilos in the world."

We went back inside and were greeted by the furnace blast of children's screams. One of the Planet Kids employees, using a wireless headset microphone, shouted orders for a group of the younger children to follow, like the leader of a cult. He wore a bright yellow shirt. It was some kind of dance sequence made up of swaying and nodding and clapping; the children seemed confused but happy. Other Planet Kids employees began arming them with red plastic balls for whatever the next phase of the game was.

"The problem is regulation," João said. "The government, they hate business, they are basically communists. In any business process, there are so many steps you have to take, because they want to make sure that their people have the opportunity to collect bribes. So you have to get this stamp, and that stamp, and for each stamp you have to pay a little extra just to make it go forward. Of course you know where the money goes."

He made a face that said he didn't have to tell me where the money goes.

Two children near us scoured the desserts table with the careful attention of truffle pigs. They selected small pink globs whose flavor I couldn't imagine and pushed them into their mouths, whole.

"They are literally buying the votes with welfare," João said. "They can never stay in power without this."

I was used to hearing Brazilians we knew—people who lived in apartments like ours—complain about the government. They needed no provocation. A gynecologist once gave me a lecture after an exam. It seemed to me that Brazilians were unusually quick to divulge political opinion, but then I thought of how easily in America you learned someone's opinion of the president. I'd met a lot more Republicans since the election of a Democrat.

Waiters circled with more meat, more beer, like vultures who forced you to eat; they had sharp eyes for empty hands. The adults were as well-tended as the children. I saw some of the men drinking whiskey. João accepted a chicken wing and, brandishing it, made another point about the president.

People I didn't know came up to say hello to him, and the conversation migrated into Portuguese. One of them, a man, turned to me and introduced himself.

I asked if he was a friend of João's. João turned to us briefly, laughing, and said something in Portuguese that meant nothing to me.

In Portuguese, the man asked what I did, who I knew.

"My husband, he is work at the bank, we have the eight months here."

"I, day, all the cars, nineteen," he said.

"Are you watching him, the game of soccer, there are the teams?"

"I speak English," the man said, in English.

I found myself alone again. My husband wasn't anywhere that I could see, and I stopped looking for him. I wandered through the near-Caligulan ruination of the party—the whining music, the carnival barking of instructions over a loudspeaker, the horror-movie shadows cast by the Batmen and the Hulks, the dinosaurs—and realized that merely being there was proof I belonged among these people. Despite the fact that it was a children's party, all the children seemed to have disappeared, having absconded perhaps to some other realm of Planet Kids with the man in the yellow shirt. The children's parents were gathered into hives dense with conversation; for them, this was a political occasion, a business opportunity. The party now was many hours old, but the tables of food, which the staff was almost surreptitiously replenishing, looked as they had at the start, giving an impression of ceaseless bounty. I sensed the party becoming a darker, uglier thing, amid the distant screams of children and tinny pop music, the deepening inebriation of the adults, the way you notice the temperature in a room has changed only after the fact. I punted a balloon that had fallen to the floor. I ate grapes. I stepped outside to get away from it all, but the party was overflowing the building, and men stood around on the sidewalk, drinking from little glasses of beer and smoking cigars. Evening had lowered itself onto the city; it was early afternoon when we'd arrived. I was shocked by how much time had passed. The party showed no sign of relenting. The valets were huddled at their station in what looked like conspiracy.

I went back inside and ate more grapes and spoke to another man I didn't know about his profession.

"My work is clichés," he said.

This, I thought, was me finally going insane.

Seeing my confusion, he explained that the word referred to stereotype printing: he created the logos and designs on packaging.

I told him that an interest of mine was phrases that seem like clichés but aren't quite: *notable absence* or *desperate rebellion*, *absolute disaster*, *unseasonably warm*. This didn't appear to entice him as a subject of conversation, either because I had no examples to give in his own language, or simply because I had managed to steer us away from the topic of work.

Iara wandered over with caipirinhas in her hands.

"I don't know if I can have anything else to drink," I said.

I had lost count of what was already inside me, already flowing through my bloodstream.

Iara said, "Are you pregnant?"

"No," I said. "Did you think I was?"

"You have been here many months, you have no job, you don't have enough to do. For a woman, a wife, the usual thing is to become pregnant."

Marcos and Iara had two daughters. They were somewhere else at the party, eating cakes, having their nails painted, riding an indoor roller coaster, bouncing in an inflatable castle with crowns on their heads.

"You should do it," Iara said. "You should have a baby."

"Is that what I should do?"

There I was, drinking the caipirinha after all.

Iara said, "You think I am joking, but I'm serious—it would solve your problem."

"My problem?"

"And men," she said. "Men expect that we will do this for them, make babies. Even when they are not thinking it, they are thinking it."

I said, "Do you have parties like this for your daughters on their birthdays?"

"Oh, you have to," she said.

Marcos came up to Iara from behind. He wrapped his arms around her and grinned at me over her shoulder.

I said, "Have you seen my husband?"

"Forever ago," he said.

INCIDENTALS

Italy; traveling.

Ravenna, the fourth city in a week. Everyone is tired. I'm tired. Tom—a friend of the man who will become my husband—is in charge of planning. Ravenna, a city in books, important history, famous architecture, Dante's tomb.

Have you even read *The Divine Comedy*? he asks Tom on the train from Florence to Ravenna. They are old friends, friends from childhood.

Parts, sure, Tom says.

Midway through my life, says the man who will become my husband.

I woke and found myself in a dark wood, Tom finishes.

We have been living in hotels, trains. Squares with fountains, languishing in the dead Italian afternoons, the air swollen with summer heat. It seems impossible at times to find a waiter, a shopkeeper. In the piazzas, tables and chairs sit empty, umbrellas folded; birds sleep. Everywhere we go has the stillness that follows an evacuation.

Another hotel. In the lobby, I can feel the authoring presence of money: calm electronic music, tastefully muted colors, careful attention to materials, glass and burnished metal. There is a carafe of chilled water with slices of citrus and cucumber, and we all drink some. Tom's girlfriend, Kathryn, is especially thirsty. She hasn't been feeling well—the heat, the rigors of travel. She's a graduate student in literature writing a dissertation that has something to do with Eliot, Stevens, and Stein; in her mind the three writers combine in a pattern I can't understand, even after several days of listening to her talk about them. She is kind, but conversation with her is intimidating. She is preoccupied with her future, calculating the benefits and trade-offs of various tenure-track positions. Her life, even accounting for its difficulties, has signposts and measures of success that mine does not.

He touches my arm and then speaks with the desk clerk. The clerk asks for a credit card, incidentals.

Incidentals, the clerk says, pronouncing the word gently in continental English.

He takes out a credit card, and as he hands it over, I hear the background hum of his professional life.

It is my third visit to Europe. Once, a trip with my parents to England and Scotland, at the end of high school; and then Paris, during college, to improve my French.

In the past year alone he has been to London, Geneva,

Brussels, Frankfurt, and Madrid, all for work. This in addition to Beijing, Tokyo, Hong Kong.

He is calm in airports, unworried about arriving shortly before a flight, unperturbed by the mechanical sounds inside the plane during takeoff and landing, indifferent to the officials at immigration and customs.

It is all background hum.

His phone has an international plan that allows him to read and respond to business e-mails during the trip. He claims to be doing this as seldom as possible.

The first order of business in Ravenna is the Basilica di San Vitale. It is a plump, crouching thing. Tourists enter and exit, following paths marked by the tourists before them, as if by chemical scent, like ants. Tom has a camera and takes pictures, and when he offers it to Kathryn, she waves it away, interested purely in looking.

Inside, the expanding mosaic of angels on the inner bulge of the ceiling, the Byzantine elaborateness of detail. I say, Eliot wrote a poem about Ravenna.

"Lune de Miel," Kathryn says, without hesitation: she has the power of immediate recall. It is like conversing with a card catalog.

A honeymooning couple, touring Europe, I say.

But the basilica they visit isn't this one, she says. It's a different basilica, just outside Ravenna.

Which is it? Tom asks.

She says the name and Tom shakes his head, already losing interest, not on his list.

Kathryn wanders to another nave.

He comes close to say, I don't think I could take you anywhere in the world where you wouldn't be able to supply a literary reference.

This is the right thing to say. I take his hand.

Is the couple happy? he says.

The couple?

In the poem.

Not really, I say. Instead of having sex they're scratching at mosquito bites. I think Eliot's point was to show their small lives in relief against the permanence of European culture.

Sounds uplifting, he says.

By the time we leave the basilica, everyone is hungry, and we embark on the herculean task of finding something to eat in Italy in the middle of an August afternoon. In the end this means cheap pizza, served to us by a gregarious Egyptian man who narrates a condensed autobiography while we wait for slices to warm in the brick oven. He has lived in Italy for thirty years, his daughters are Italian, he loves Americans. No one talks much while we eat.

It is obvious that Kathryn wants to return to the hotel and lie down, and Tom finally suggests it.

In the room, I try to rest, without success. I don't want to be inside. He is answering work e-mails. I say I'm going for a walk, and he kisses me, barely looking up from the small laptop he uses for travel.

Tomorrow afternoon we'll take a train back to Rome, and then the flight to New York. Tom and Kathryn have a longer trip, San Francisco—she's at the University of Berkeley and he works for Google, stock options already vested—and they will spend one more night in Rome, the Eternal City.

I leave the hotel without a plan and run into Tom almost immediately.

She's sleeping, he says.

He's working, I say.

He mentions that Kathryn gave him permission to visit Dante's tomb without her.

So I follow Tom.

I find him easy to talk to. He is obviously intelligent, but wears it lightly; unlike Kathryn, he doesn't stop midsentence in search of a better or more exact word, and allows his thoughts to peddle out imperfectly, with normal human habits of cliché, lacunae.

We speak casually of the things we saw in Venice, Florence, already taking the shape of memories.

Florence and Ravenna are the cities of Dante's birth and death. They had a dispute over his bones. In Florence, a tomb stands empty, the symbol of the city's regret over the loss of its native son.

Dante died of malaria, I say.

Sure, Tom says. Italy was like Africa then.

All of Europe was, I say.

We turn a corner and step into cool shade. A little white mausoleum. We read the inscription. A small, fat man with an enormous camera hanging from his neck says something to me, first in Italian, then in Spanish. Finally he detects my incomprehension and smiles.

Thank you, he says.

We don't spend long. Tom takes a few photos. O.K., he says.

But before we start to walk away, Tom says, You can probably tell that things aren't great with Kathryn.

I don't answer. He isn't looking at me. He is looking at Dante's tomb, pretending to read the inscription again.

I'm going to talk to her once we're home, he says.

I understand that by talking to her he means ending the relationship. Tom tells me, in some detail, what's wrong. From the way he speaks, I have the sense that he's saying some of these things out loud for the first time, experimenting with how it feels to say them. Because he isn't looking at me, I return the favor, and stare at the dirty white marble of the tomb, insects there, the blocks of shade where it is hidden from the sun.

At last I ask if he's already talked about this with his friend, the man who will become my husband.

I think he would judge me, Tom says, and finally meets my eye.

I want to ask what this means, but pressing him seems out of bounds, somehow.

I'm sorry, I say instead, because it is the natural thing to say.

Tom nods.

We leave, and walk together for a while in silence, vaguely in the direction of the hotel. We pass a restaurant that is just opening. From the heat of the road, the interior looks cool and hospitable. A girl is folding cloth napkins. Tom asks if I'd like to stop for a drink.

Yes, I say.

We order a bottle of rosé. The waiter pours two glasses and plunks the bottle into a bucket of ice on a stand by the table. It becomes clear that we won't speak further about Kathryn. I understand that what Tom told me is something he expects I won't divulge. And he is right—I won't. I won't tell him, ever, what Tom said to me at Dante's tomb, even after Tom and Kathryn marry, a wedding at which my husband will give the toast, and I won't tell him even after they have a child, and then a second, in rapid succession, as Kathryn abandons her academic career in favor of motherhood, something I would have found impossible to imagine of the woman who corrected my memory of which basilica in Ravenna the couple visits in Eliot's "Lune de Miel."

A waiter refreshes our glasses before Tom can reach for the bottle. The girl who was folding napkins before now brings platters of antipasti from the kitchen and places them on the bar—cold meats, arancini, eggplant caponata, globes of baby mozzarella in oil and herbs.

Do you think it's complimentary? Tom says.

The only other customers, an older couple, rise from their table and fill plates with food from the bar. Tom and I exchange a look and then do the same. By the time we sit down, the waiter has refreshed our glasses again.

The food is delicious. I feel a deep sense of pleasure and gratitude at the almost magical appearance of this food and the insanity that it is being provided to us at no cost. For a moment the world seems generous. More platters come out from the kitchen.

We wonder aloud at the propriety of taking seconds, thirds, and then we do it anyway, scooping piles of food indecently onto the little appetizer plates.

Tom is laughing, I'm laughing, the waiter smiles as he empties the last of the wine into our glasses, indulging us.

And then Tom is telling me about a party at someone's apartment on the Upper East Side.

This was when I still lived in New York, he says, before you guys were dating.

We went out a lot, he says.

Tom tells me that at this party on the Upper East Side they saw Salman Rushdie, fresh off his most recent divorce, hitting on women in their twenties and eating a sandwich.

So they were at a party, in this story. They were peripheral guests, friends of the friend of someone else's friend. An exclusive party that wasn't in reality very exclusive. I sense the solidity, the full shape, of the memory behind the sketch Tom is giving.

The way Rushdie was holding that sandwich, Tom says, holding it with his hand at his waist, while he talked to a woman—I mean, crumbs were falling on the floor.

I laugh and say, He writes like a man who would let crumbs fall to the floor.

Kathryn was there, he says. And Kendra was, he adds, as if surprising himself. Kendra, I realize, is an old girlfriend, and after a moment I even remember the name, mentioned once, in passing, then forgotten.

For a moment, Tom is silent, and I wait to see if he will say more.

You aren't like the girls he used to date, Tom says.

And then the conversation drifts in another direction, and then it is too late to ask what he means by this.

The bill comes and Tom waves me off, hands the waiter some euros, and then we return to the hotel, the heat of the day finally relenting. In the room, I expect to find him still on his laptop, but he is lying on the bed. He seems to have been waiting for my return. He asks what I've been up to, and I tell him about the food, and apologize for being tipsy, and he laughs and kisses me. The sensation of lips mixes with the wine in my blood, and suddenly I want sex, and I move a hand into the waist of his pants before noticing a strange expression on his face, one I can't quite interpret, and then I see the ice bucket with the neck of a bottle sticking out, a crown of gold foil.

Oh, I say.

And then, because of all the afternoon's activity, it is almost ten o'clock when we are sitting down to dinner. Over the first sips of wine the conversation is entirely consumed with Kathryn's and Tom's admiration of the ring, asking where he bought it, what was my reaction, what was going through my mind. I say that I probably said yes because Tom had gotten me drunk already, and we all laugh, and while the others are laughing I realize that he surely would have told Tom beforehand, he would have showed his oldest friend the ring; even though I bumped into Tom that afternoon seemingly at random, I begin to wonder if it was all part of a plan, Tom keeping me away from the hotel so that I could return and be surprised. I have been drinking for hours and know I am drunk, but the feeling is safe, pleasant, nothing more than the inner radiation of emotion. We recount the stations of the trip, a little nostalgic already, our week of vacation coming to an end, punctuated by the proposal. I study Tom, his face as he turns toward Kathryn, but see no trace there of what he confessed to me.

We order mindlessly, cheeses, vegetables marinated in oil, pastas, fish and meat. Everyone eats from everyone else's plate. It is a day and night already breaking apart into vivid blotches of memory, like stains on a white tablecloth, and I realize I am talking quite a bit, enjoying the lapidary construction of sentences, syntax itself more pleasurable to my wine-excited brain than the actual content of the sentences. I laugh. Who else does this, I think, who else talks merely for the sensation of words snapping together, resolving miraculously into structures, into the beautiful architecture of sentences. I manage to stop talking and let conversation swirl around me. Waiters go by in black shirts, black pants. Espressos drop onto the table, someone has gelato. Then the bill comes, handwritten, thin paper on a metal tray. I feel the men reaching for their wallets. No, I say, no, I want to buy everyone dinner, it's our last night, this is my treat, I say, even as I am fumbling in my purse for money, I am a woman engaged to be married.

That's O.K., he says.

His wallet is open. Tom's wallet is open.

No, really, I want to, I say. I realize that I haven't looked at the bill and have no idea how much it is.

You shouldn't, he says, more quietly.

We can split it, Tom says.

I feel the glance that passes between the men.

I haven't paid for a thing all week, I say. I want to pay for something. I want to use my money.

My voice—I hear it. It is emotional. It is too much. But it is something now I can't control. They all hear it as well, and their hands retreat from the tray with the bill. They think perhaps I will come to my senses, agree to share the cost, but in a single motion I pick up the bill, fold it around my credit card, and hand it to the waiter.

There, I say. There.

But I already know what is going to happen. The waiter is going to tell me that the restaurant accepts only cash, because this is Italy, and I, who don't have nearly enough euros to cover the bill, will be forced to relent, and my companions will act as if this isn't a humiliation, as if nothing has happened, and I will try to play along, I—a woman engaged to be married and drunk on Italian wine—will insist nevertheless on emptying my wallet of what's there, not more than forty or fifty euros, and the man who will become my husband will mix it with his money, Tom's money, organizing it by denomination, counting and recounting, and then he will say, as the others begin to stand, chairs scraping against the tile, he will say, I think we're good.

THE DISASTER OF HETEROSEXUALITY

Marcos said the protests, the outbreak of popular discontent, confirmed his long-held view of things. "Brazilians are tired of the usual politics," he said. Later I mentioned our conversation to Iara. She made a face.

There was a lot of opinion out there about Brazilians. This was opinion that lived in its natural habitat, the Internet. The opinions seemed to belong to people who had spent a week in Rio on vacation and now considered themselves experts—the Internet being the natural habitat, also, of experts.

> Brazilians bring a certain flair to the way they express themselves. Brazilians are friendly and free-spirited. Brazilians are comfortable in their own skin. Brazilians are so nationalistic and arrogant. Brazilians love fireworks. Brazilians love children. Brazilians are extremely

> devout. Brazilians eat a much more balanced diet than a lot of Europeans/North Americans. Brazilians have mastered a way to bend the rules to accommodate their needs. Brazilians tend to live life at a slower pace, and this carries over into business. Not all Brazilian women are extremely hot. Some are just hot.

I would say that the average Brazilian weighs what the average American weighs. And I'd estimate that the percentage of Brazilians who are exceptionally attractive is comparable to the percentage of Nigerians who make a living from e-mail scams.

Which is not to discount the fact that living in Brazil felt different from living in America. That being among Brazilians felt different from being among Americans. That there was a lot of cheek-kissing. That the physical element of everyday conversation was significant, the incidence of touching in everyday conversation. That Brazilians indulged their children to an aberrant degree, and were loath to scold them. That Brazilians really did run a lot of red lights, and I heard fireworks in our neighborhood almost daily.

When you're a foreigner, it's difficult to resist that kind of thinking altogether, categorical thinking. Brazilians are. Brazilians do. Brazilians believe.

"That's because Italians are just Brazilians who were born in Europe!" said a man as he touched my shoulder, and then, for good measure, my elbow. He was a Brazilian who was born in Brazil.

I asked for a coffee with milk. The waitress stared at me as if I hadn't said anything. I spoke the words again; and still the waitress stared. I waited. I tried once more, a coffee with milk. They were the simplest words. A brief moment went by. Then the waitress walked away. I didn't know if this meant she had understood me, and would bring me a coffee with milk, or if she had given up.

Sundays in our neighborhood were market days. Vendors piled up great lordly mounds of tropical fruit, brightly glowing, still wet—papayas, mangos, watermelons, pineapples, kiwis, bananas. There was star fruit, cashew fruit, passion fruit, dragon fruit. Every man had a knife in his hand, and as you walked past he sliced off the flesh of the nearest thing, and bade you to eat it.

Friendship overseas was tenuous. You exchanged intimacies right at the start, and then one person or the other clammed up, slipped away. People were promiscuous with the word *friend*; they used it to describe fucking everybody. The constant drinking surely played a role in all this. People disappeared. Other people turned up. One of the Wives, someone I never would have guessed, was twice divorced.

Day—from an Old English word that also means "day" but can mean "lifetime" as well, and from the Sanskrit *dah*, "to burn."

I was seeing Iara more often. The time I spent with Iara was distinct from the time I spent with Marcos at our lessons. Each of them was a hemisphere; only one rotated into view at a time. Iara mentioned Marcos more often than Marcos mentioned Iara. "I'm not the kind of woman who waits around," Iara would say, apropos or not.

My husband was generally very good with informational empathy. He didn't use potentially unfamiliar names as if the person listening should know them, and he had a strong instinct for which facts the listener would recognize and which needed context. It's the sort of trait you don't notice until someone else does the opposite; and most people do the opposite. He was good in English with nonnative speakers, operating in an idiom that didn't sound infantile, and also wouldn't confuse his listener. He knew what was colloquialism and what wasn't. He was sure-handed, in other words. But he never betrayed moral anxiety. He was sure of what he was sure of.

"I think the plant is dying."

"The one we bought three weeks ago? It's dying already?"

"Look at the leaves. See—yellow."

"Maybe it needs more water. This could be reversible. I'm getting some water."

"Don't you think it's not a good sign that we can't even keep a plant alive? What did the woman at the store say? 'Requires almost no care'?"

We met at a party, Manhattan, someone's apartment. We spoke for a while, and eventually I went home, and later the poet I was sort of dating came over. We had sex, and then we smoked cigarettes on the fire escape and shared a bottle of beer, and he asked me how the night was, and I didn't say anything about the party. Years later I would remember smoking with the poet on the fire escape, the view of other buildings, other fire escapes, the feeling of New York City late at night, the feeling of being young. There was nothing consequential about that part of the evening, but for some reason it survived as memory. It's possible that the memory of smoking on the fire escape with the poet comes from a different night, not the night I met the man who would become my husband, but I wouldn't know, so firmly do I now associate the two events in my mind.

It occurred to me that you could put it another way: *There will be more past in the future.*

A word might have an unknown origin. *Bludgeon*, *hunker*, *slang*, *dog*, *flummox*. It was one of those things, like an island without people, that could seem either beautiful or sinister.

"No, not the restaurant in Paris. I'm thinking of the restaurant in Lyon, the one where we ate the second night, not the first night."

"The one with a chandelier made of Coke bottles?"

"No, the other one."

"Then I don't remember it. I really thought the Coke-bottle chandelier place was the second night."

"Actually, I think the chandelier was made of wineglasses."

"Really?"

"Anyway, whichever it was, we had the exact same conversation there. And you said something totally different then."

"There and then. I really did think that was the Coke bottle–wineglass chandelier place, the second night."

"That part doesn't matter."

"Don't you think two people's memories should complement one another, not cancel each other out?"

The Haitian refugees at the church told me their stories. I helped where I could, I sympathized. I initially had the idea that I might come to know some of them individually, but that wasn't really how it worked.

There was an Angolan man, tall, with a round, soft face, soft lips. The upper shell of his forehead shined with sweat where the hair had fallen out. The man's name was Boaventura, and he'd worked with Padre Piero for two years. He was in essence Padre Piero's lieutenant. He organized the new arrivals, sorted out problems with the kitchen staff. He performed lowly errands, and he was the only other man who had a key to Padre Piero's office. He was once a refugee himself.

I assumed he stayed with the church, helping other refugees, out of a sense of duty, the desire to do good works. I assumed he was a Christian. This wasn't the case.

I don't have anything to say to God, he said. You want to know why I stay with the church. In any job I seek, people are going to look down on me, an African, but here at the church I am always less of a refugee than the new refugees you see here.

I saw what he meant. The newcomers looked at Boaventura as a man who had something to offer. He had a kind of status. Brazil is like your country, he said, a country of immigrants. For many people it is a destination. But my plan was never to go from one colony to another. One day I am going to live in America.

Boaventura used an alloy of Portuguese, scrapyard English, and some patois he picked up from the Haitians. He liked the phrase "the pursuit of happiness." He always wore a baseball cap, the Yankees.

I was a powerful man in Angola, I had money. My family was involved in oil. We made enemies inside the government, and I saw how unstable it was, how fast it was going to happen. My money was in the wrong banks. In my country you can't have faith in what you own. That whole story, how we lost what we had, now it seems like a single chapter in a much longer book. This book is still being written. One day Brazil will be like that for me, a single chapter, a paragraph, when I am living in America.

If I cannot go to America, I will go to London.

For Boaventura, it was necessary that I believe his story, both his account of the past and his account of the future—that I believe he was once a man of importance in Luanda and would be important again. That he was something more than the man I was seeing: a refugee. I wanted to say, I believe you. But saying it aloud would have convinced him that I did not believe him, and then he would have resented me.

I saw Boaventura washing himself at the sink. He slowly cleaned his hands, his forearms, his face, and the back of his neck, like a Muslim performing ablutions. He scooped water into his mouth and rinsed, and then he washed the Yankees hat, wringing it out before replacing it on his head.

It's easy for sympathy to become condescending, of course; but empathy can turn to condescension as well. Then you're really stuck.

Luciano wandered into the kitchen during a lesson with Claudia.

"My son, he shows his face," Claudia announced. "Luciano, be polite, say hello."

"Hello," he said, and drank a glass of juice.

"You know, he has changed the passwords on his phone and his e-mail," Claudia said after he left.

My husband and I boarded a plane and flew south—Florianópolis, an island city that a few years earlier people had started calling the new Ibiza. I don't think the label stuck. People are always looking for the new something when the old something becomes too expensive, too crowded, too familiar. Florianópolis wasn't Ibiza, but it was very nice.

We spent hours in bed, fucking, dozing, drinking bottles of champagne delivered to the room, watching movies—it was that kind of vacation. We slept late and then took long naps in the afternoon; all that drinking and non-procreative sex was exhausting, apparently.

It was also a way of avoiding the subject of procreative sex. The trip felt like the reenactment of a time in our marriage before the question of children arose, a time when such questions still belonged to the future.

Late in the day, we would head down to the beach, passing through the private access/egress provided by the hotel, to the narrow skirt of sand along the water's edge. The noise of the Atlantic Ocean was surprisingly gentle. All that size and power, reduced to a comforting susurrus.

We didn't agonize over where to eat dinner, we just wandered into a restaurant and ordered too much seafood and ate greedily, then went back to the room and had more sex. Then we slept again.

We didn't do anything cultural—no churches, no museums. We learned nothing about the place we were visiting. It was the kind of vacation in which you board an airplane in order to be in a room that's different from the room you're normally in. I usually think of pleasure as something that's supposed to be complicated.

Clubs—the one thing we did in Florianópolis aside from eating and sex. Clubs sat at the edge of the beach like boat landings, open to the water, pillowed white chairs on the boardwalks, candles on the tables, fairy lights outside, black ocean. We weren't alone. All around us were schools of lounging bodies—moneyed Brazilians and Argentines, Uruguayans—everyone on their portables, racking up page views, likes, posting images of the night scenery, choosing filters, taking more selfies and group shots. All of this was less stupid than it looked; it was life. The speakers played David Guetta and Calvin Harris and Rihanna. They were names I was used to thinking of as ephemeral, in a way that Beethoven and Mozart and Bach were not. But Rihanna's music was surely heard by a larger fraction of the world's population than Bach's ever was in his lifetime, a fraction that quite possibly included more people than the whole of the world's population when Bach was alive. We danced. The lyrics of that kind of music weren't supposed to matter, but I found myself seduced anyway by the promise at the heart of those songs—that pleasure was inherently disposable, that the enjoyment of disposable pleasure was the only enjoyment life really offered, that life was nothing more than one disposable moment after another, and if life had a point, it was to ensure that as many of those disposable moments as possible were pleasure, not pain. Those songs said: Don't make it harder than it has to be.

On our last day in Florianópolis, I realized I was happy, and I knew that any more time there would ruin the effect. Vacation—something enjoyable in small doses that in any larger dose would become unbearable.

Somewhere on the Internet I read that Florianópolis was once called Nossa Senhora do Desterro—Our Lady of Banishment. Good thing they changed it. That isn't the way to sell the new Ibiza.

When you flew into the airport after a period of time away, São Paulo seemed to have grown. I was surprised by a feeling almost like nostalgia, a feeling of missing something that wasn't yet gone, because I knew that whatever else was true about it, it wouldn't last forever.

The plane descended toward the airport along the flight path I could see from our apartment window. I looked for our building; but the buildings all looked the same. I couldn't make the sighting in reverse—couldn't see myself watching from our apartment as the plane descended.

I saw the boy who spoke English in our building's elevator. I said hello. He began asking questions. Where are your children? Are they in America? What city are you from?

Iara turned up at my apartment toward the end of a lesson with Fabiana, and immediately they were seized with conversation; Brazilians who had known each other for minutes could seem like blood relatives. Iara had arrived blooming with shopping bags and from one of them produced a bottle of sparkling pink wine. Fabiana stayed for lunch. Soon the two of them were discussing a retrospective of Hélio Oiticica's sculpture, and then a recent exhibition of Lygia Clark's work; Banco do Brasil maintained a cultural center downtown that put on first-rate shows: one of the exhibition spaces was inside the old bank vault. And then it was the traffic caused by road work on Avenida José Diniz. Then the general political situation. They mostly spoke English, for my benefit, and when they switched to Portuguese, Fabiana would touch my arm and say, "Vamos, uma lição." Iara loved that. She said she found Marcos's politics increasingly unpleasant. "He thinks businessmen should be in charge of the country." They asked about my husband's views. "I think my husband and I have basically the same politics," I said.

"Then what is it?"

"What?"

"There is always something," Iara said.

After a moment, I said: "Differences of sensibility, maybe."

It came up that Fabiana had worked as a journalist for a while.

"Everyone works as a journalist at some point," Iara said.

Fabiana mentioned the name of the magazine.

"Fascists," Iara said.

Fabiana nodded in agreement, then said: "But what can we do? What else do we have?"

"I'm watching T.V."

"Yeah."

"There are literally six different soccer matches going on right now."

"Yeah."

"Oh, I found the news. It's another protest. Can you see it from your office? I can't tell where this one is."

"I don't see anything. It's probably on Paulista."

"People look angry."

"They're protestors. They're angry."

"It seems like this is serious, the protests. It doesn't seem like it's going to stop anytime soon."

"Yeah."

"Are you coming home soon?"

"I just have to finish this thing."

"The signs look like the ones I saw last time. Do you think they recycle the signs? They must. There's a guy dressed as a skeleton."

"Listen, I have to go."

On the matter of procreation I did not feel what my husband felt. I did not feel the native urge that most women felt, supposedly. I saw only complication, peril. I saw Luciano, the boy who was failing his tests and sequestered in his room watching revolution porn on the Internet. I saw the impoverished boys who robbed us. I saw the difficulty ahead for all of them. The rich housewives whose nannies spent more time with their kids than they did—every argument sounded trite once it came out of my mouth, but this didn't undo the strength of my feelings. Children seemed inherently fraught to me, reproduction, the whole species, the planetary consequences. Having children wasn't in my mind an act of selflessness, but rather one of enormous selfishness: the making of a creature whose existence is entirely your fault and who has to bear the costs of your decision; and this is not to mention the costs society bears. I thought of the weaknesses every person has, the unmet desires, the confusion, the anxiety, the pain, the personal inconsistency, the incoherent striving, the dependence on animal pleasures and material distraction. I wasn't sold. I worried that any child would turn out to be the victim of something, or the perpetrator. My husband didn't see it this way; he couldn't understand why I did. Are *we* victims? Are *we* perpetrators? He became exasperated when I used the word *species*. We're not talking about the species, he said, we're talking about the two of us, two people. "But that's how a species happens," I said. They were awful fights, truly awful, sometimes.

An e-mail from Helen:

> I'm absolutely convinced I know less than I did five years ago. Certainly less than I did when I graduated from college. Is it possible I reached the peak of my intelligence when I was twenty-two years old? I still have

a copy of *Malone Dies* from that comparative lit class you forced me to take senior year. Notes in the margins! Who wrote those? Now they might as well be Cyrillic. If I read the book now, I would write: Why does Beckett hate paragraph breaks? Why does Beckett hate *me*? If I had gone to grad school instead of going straight to work, I would feel less ignorant, but I would also have less money. Men in D.C. come in three types: lawyers, government bureaucrats, and congressional staffers. They might all be lawyers, actually. They talk about work to the exclusion of everything else, to a degree I did not think possible, and I came here from New York. I was so certain it was time to go. Now I miss it. Isn't that funny?

At the church a young woman removed toast from the toaster and proceeded to butter it on both sides. This was in the small kitchen on the second floor. I had never seen anyone actually do such a thing, butter one side of the bread and then the other.

Her name was Hannah. She was a graduate student of some kind, American, living in Brazil to do research, and her research had led her to the church. She was the only other affiliated American. The most interesting thing about what she was doing with the bread was that, having buttered both sides, she nevertheless attempted to hold it in such a way that her fingers didn't become greasy. That was the tricky part.

"Jean-Pierre was telling me about his family in Port-au-Prince," Hannah said. "He has three daughters. He is worried they will become prostitutes. I asked if he ever went to prostitutes. He didn't lie. He said he went sometimes. I asked if his wife knew. I asked if he got tested. He was very offended. Of course he didn't talk to his wife about that sort of thing. What kind of man did I think he was?"

Jean-Pierre was having trouble finding work. Hannah believed it was an issue of temperament. She heard him speaking with the recruiters. He was obstinate, he didn't seem to want the work being offered, even though the recruiters demanded no qualifications, really; they only wanted someone to act pleased about being hired. I asked what sort of work he wanted.

"He wants to work in America. He has a brother in New York. He looks at Brazil and he sees a station stop, not a destination. I think the coyotes who brought him here lied to him. They let him believe he'd be in the States in the end." Hannah finished the toast. "Five years ago, these guys would have been dying in boats, trying to reach Florida, and now they're hiking through the jungle to Brazil. The government here gives them papers, status. It's not a bad deal. You can see that immigration patterns in the Western Hemisphere are changing. It seemed perfect for my research. And now—I'm having difficulty with Jean-Pierre. I have difficulty with the question of men like Jean-Pierre."

Hannah was unwithholding with talk. I learned that initially her research topic had been sex workers in the Northeast of Brazil, but for vague reasons that line of inquiry had petered out, and after a period of indecision, she turned her attention to immigrant populations. Casually she alluded to throwing out months or even years of work. Hannah appeared to be a woman who was comfortable with directionlessness. At one point, she had taken a break from research and found work in a pizzeria in some beach town. She was in Brazil on a student visa, so this was not strictly legal, and she mentioned running into some trouble with the authorities. "But it worked out," she said. A very Brazilian way of putting it, I couldn't help but think.

The state orchestra gave a performance at which they played Stravinsky's *Firebird* suite, and for an encore the conductor returned to the stage and led the musicians through the finale a second time—it took me a moment to realize that the music I was hearing was the music I'd just heard. Outside it was windy, and thin bodies huddled at the edge of the plaza. They were smoking crack. I saw small, trembling flames in the pipes; smoke seemed to grow from their mouths. Police were everywhere in gray bulletproof vests. Only as my husband and I were getting into a taxi did I notice the spray paint on the entrance of the concert hall. *Queimar os ricos*. Burn the rich, that is. Later I learned that a group of protestors had attempted to enter the concert hall during the performance; the police turned them back. No one told those of us inside while this was happening.

According to the newspapers the protests were growing larger because the middle class was now involved.

Someone's remark on the protestors: "Those children are the children of the rich." And so the arguments went in circles.

João gestured with a cigarette. He approved of the protests, he said. It was long past time for Brazilians to speak out about the government's corruption, malfeasance, degradation. I knew that João hadn't approved of the protests initially; he'd found the premise childish. They want all the buses to be free, he'd said. Who do they think will pay? I asked why he approved of the protests now. No, he said, it's good, people should express themselves, it's one of our freedoms. João was already lighting another cigarette. The government has to know how the people feel.

At dinner Brazilians smoked, or at least the Brazilians I knew smoked. We ate in restaurants with gardens, courtyards. We dined outdoors even when the weather was cool. Indoors there were candles, old mirrors; sometimes there were fountains, vines climbing the walls. I knew who had visited Rio lately. I knew who had beach houses on São Paulo's northern shore, I knew how many bedrooms they had.

Tergiversate: an obscure word in English that means to change one's mind repeatedly with regard to a given subject, even to change one's loyalty. The word has a connotation of cowardice and betrayal that *equivocate* and *prevaricate* don't quite match. It is a word too seldom used, if only because of its obvious applications. *Tergiversate* has a Portuguese cognate, and the two words share a Latin root. The Latin root means "to turn one's back."

I was watching Rossellini's *Journey to Italy* when my husband came home. It was already late. He joined me on the sofa. He didn't ask what the movie was, the plot. After a while he got up to fetch a beer. The husband and wife in the film were having an argument. From the doorway he pointed at the bottle in his hand as a way of asking if I wanted one, too.

I did ridiculous things occasionally. For instance, I bought a piece of salmon from the fishmonger at the Sunday market because I liked the idea of being the kind of woman who buys fresh salmon at the market and then cooks it for dinner. But I was certain before I was even halfway home that I would never use it. The fish sat in the refrigerator for five days, diligently rotting, before I put the stinking carcass out with the trash. The next time I did this, I tossed the fish in a garbage can on the street on my way home, as a way of improving efficiency, and I told myself that it was really no different from purchasing a doorstop of a novel you know in your heart you will never read.

"But it's not like we're going to live in Brazil forever. It makes no sense to think about it in those terms."

"I was under the impression that we were going to live here for a while."

"Maybe for a while. It depends on what you and I want."

"What we want. That's a good question. What do we want?"

"That's what I'm trying to say. What *do* you want?"

"If I have a kid, then I'm just a woman who has a kid."

"The word for that is mother," he said.

I found myself telling Hannah about the robbery. I did this while also working with one of the Haitian men on his paperwork. I was dwelling, I told Hannah, on the fact that I wouldn't have noticed the boys who robbed us if they hadn't robbed us. I told her I didn't believe it was traumatic, this wasn't why I was dwelling on the robbery, but I couldn't stop thinking about it.

"I've been robbed three times since coming to São Paulo. I was with a friend the last time. There were two guys, and the guy who was robbing my friend clearly knew what he was doing. He got my friend's iPhone, all his money. My guy wasn't as experienced. He was like an intern, like a mugger intern. An experienced guy would have just taken the purse. Instead this guy's looking through my purse while we're standing in the street, asking me what do I have, what do I have. And I'm like, What do you *want*, man? He ended up with a few bills and missed the four hundred *dollars* sitting at the bottom," Hannah said.

She spoke about what happened to her in the way I wished I could speak about what happened to me. She was witty, good humored, relaxed; she manipulated the story into comedy. Hannah spoke about the mugging—her three muggings—as just another episode of life. She was laughing; she gave the impression that she had been laughing even while the robbery took place, laughing as the mugger intern did a beginner's job of mugging her.

"He was still building his résumé," I said.

I went out at night. Iara was at Bar Ritz with friends; she kissed me on both cheeks when I arrived. I knew some of the people with her, some I didn't. My husband was working late. Iara seemed always to have some rich friends with her and some artist friends. They had come from an event. Everyone was laughing. I ordered a glass of wine and began to gather strands of meaning from the Portuguese being spoken around me. Iara leaned into my ear and asked what Marcos and my husband were doing. "Doing? He's still at work," I said. Something happened at the corners of Iara's eyes. Then she looked away and said, "I thought maybe I would see Marcos here. I know it is a place he likes."

I read an article by a feminist who out of nowhere referred to "the disaster of heterosexuality." It went more or less unexplained, this provocation, unelaborated upon; it was left to stand on its own, the way you would write "glass ceiling" and assume your reader knew what you meant. I searched online to see if "the disaster of heterosexuality" was standard in a subfield of academic thought, the way "queer poetics" or "symbolic interactionism" is. I found it nowhere else. But I couldn't shake the phrase from my mind; it glowed with life. I saw the rich idea gestating within "the disaster of heterosexuality"—heterosexuality being the means by which we reproduce as a species, as human beings, by which we accumulate more of ourselves, and thus create war, ethnic hatred, standardized tests, profit-and-loss, status updates, top-ten lists, genital mutilation, A.T.M. surcharges, native advertising, Black Friday, Pumpkin Spice Pringles, radioactive waste, global warming, everything.

"I keep thinking about where they sleep."

It was late, I couldn't blot out the glare of thought.

"Seems like they mostly work nights," he said.

"I'm sure they don't have beds, not beds in the sense that you and I have a bed. They don't have blackout curtains, extra pillows, a white-noise machine. You've seen the favelas. It has to be loud, stinking, always too hot or too cold."

"You aren't obligated to empathize with the kids who robbed us. You really don't know anything about their lives. I *haven't* seen the favelas. *You* haven't seen the favelas."

"They must never be able to sleep. They must always be so fucking exhausted."

YOU HAVE TO BE ABLE TO EXPLAIN WHAT THE GINI COEFFICIENT IS

Almost daily, it seemed, there was news of another protest. No one knew how far it would go, where it was heading. The newspapers wrote in historic terms, in terms of making history. The size and persistence of the crowds, the resonance of their demands: something in the country had to change. Everything now seemed important. The scope of what was happening. The way people were talking. There was a feeling of electric uncertainty, of endings unwritten. One night a group attacked a Santander bank, a Mercedes-Benz dealership. They destroyed several cars and savaged an A.T.M. Police tore into crowds with rubber bullets, bombed them with tear gas. I told myself this was the country where I lived, the city. The major dailies disagreed about the cost of the damage to the Mercedes-Benz dealership.

"It annoys me, people who bitch about the end of things—the end of bookstores, the end of travel agencies, the end of newspapers, the end of, I don't know, some language no one speaks anymore. As if we're the first people who watched things end. Doesn't every century have the last of something? The last Neanderthal, the last bohemian, the last pygmy rhino. It's just time. There was a last Neanderthal for a reason. Time demolishes stuff. Time happens," my husband said, demolishing some wine himself.

"Vinyl records are popular again," I said. He drank, and said, "Lazarus." He laughed. He touched the bottle at the level of the wine to indicate how far it had fallen, as one example, I supposed, of marking time; the night had started with a full bottle, and martinis before that. He laughed.

"Time doesn't make things old. Time makes things new," he said.

Claudia said Luciano was becoming secretive. She was finding things. She found masks, firecrackers, cans of spray paint. He said he was holding them for friends. This didn't mollify her. She evidently wasn't concerned about invading the privacy of an adult male as a matter of course. Brazilians by custom will live at home with their parents until they marry, until they are twenty-seven, twenty-eight years old, knocking on the door of thirty. Although of course many Brazilians also marry young.

I read the newspapers. Information began to accumulate. Young people were disappointed with politics. Many of Iara's artist friends said they saw no difference between the two main rivals, the Workers' Party and the Brazilian Social Democracy Party, everyone was corrupt, it was all part of the same system. I asked Fabiana for her views. She said that party was once identity—you saw tattoos on the arms of older Brazilians—but that this was slipping away. I thought of Luciano, unaffiliated, angry, bored by the future. He saw no choices. He was a rich boy but in this way was no different from the boys in the favelas. The difference was that Luciano surely would not be punished for his mistakes, and so he was determined to make them.

There was talk of 1984—the year the military dictatorship collapsed. Mass protests and labor strikes brought down the regime, people in the streets, pressure from below. Brazil was a young democracy, everyone said.

The newspapers were fascinated by a group calling itself Black Blocs. Supposedly this group was infiltrating the protests and causing mayhem. They had a Facebook page; the Facebook page proved that anarchists were as fluent in emoticons as everybody else. They were inspired by namesakes from the past—West Germany in the 1980s, the Seattle W.T.O. riots. They were young, university students, high school kids. I read one article in which the reporter claimed she had spoken with a fourteen-year-old. It was the Black Blocs who attacked the banks and the car dealerships. A politics of broken glass. The police took special interest. There were rumors that the Black Blocs had formed an alliance with the country's most notorious prison gang. The anarchists organized over the Internet: no leaders, no required reading.

There was a rumor about vinegar: a cloth soaked in vinegar would protect you from the tear gas. People were arrested for having bottles of vinegar, I heard, or read. When I asked Claudia if she had found bottles of vinegar in Luciano's room, she only stared back at me, confused, maybe thinking she didn't know the word I had just used, although the English was a cognate of the Portuguese.

Claudia, perhaps because of the housekeeper, was comfortable with the idea of other people being inside the apartment while she was not. She was always dashing off to attend to one of her children.

And so I had another chance to talk to Luciano. "I read something in the newspaper about the Black Blocs," I said. He said, "The newspapers don't tell the truth. The police provoke the violence. The people don't provoke the violence."

He was a teenager, a boy, and I thought how pure everything must have felt inside him. I wanted to tell him it's funny what you believe so ferociously when you're young, ferociously enough to commit stupid acts, such as putting on a mask and picking fights with police. It's not that what you believe changes, or completely disappears; it's that it fades, like paint fades. Like paint—in exactly the same dull, predictable, universal way. And the few people for whom it doesn't fade are, let's face it, completely unbearable.

Why do you feel this way? Is it because at seventeen you have lost faith already in your government? Is it because the rich have too much power, because the poor have no voice? Is it because the class system in your country is too rigid? Is it because the police provoke the violence, because the very presence of police is a form of violence, part of a system controlled by the state and designed to protect the status of wealth? Is it because doormen have to act happy about holding doors? Is it because under capitalism free will is nothing more than the engine of profit? Is it because the entire point of capitalism is to turn human beings and the choices we make into disposable units of value?

Claudia would be home any minute, and I would become the tutor again. We would look for refinements.

My mother doesn't see that people are suffering, because the only suffering she knows is medical suffering. She knows what to give someone to relieve physical pain. But she doesn't understand that people need other kinds of relief. What I feel, I can't explain to her, to anyone. She has only one idea of life. My friends don't know, my girlfriend. Her dream is to visit New York City.

I'm sure your mother only wants you to be happy and safe, I said, or words to that effect.

"Really—can you name even one of your great-grandmothers?"

"I can name them all. Marie, Nancy, Glenda, Flo. Flo was for Florence."

"Marie."

"She was French, born in France."

"You know all this about her. Do you remember her?"

"Glasses of lemonade, the porch in summer, bacon sandwiches. I don't think I've ever asked about your great-grandparents."

"Why would you? I have no idea."

"My mother keeps a book."

"I become anxious when the bank wants me to use my maternal grandmother's maiden name as an online security question. Who actually knows that sort of thing? Shut up. I know you know."

"Kincaid," he said.

I was raised in Massachusetts. I had loving, intelligent parents who were occasionally aloof, or simply missed the point. But no fights. What do I recall? The slow, deep summers, passing like glaciers. The bite and raw silence of winter. Massachusetts children remember seasons. When my husband talked about childhood, he talked about his brothers, what he and his brothers did together, the battles.

Iara knew a man called Washington who made conceptual art about barriers. For instance: a sculpture in which glass shards bristle up from a plaster foundation, inspired by the makeshift security of people who can't afford to install razor wire. My husband and I went to Washington's show, at a gallery on Praça Benedito Calixto. The gallery was loud, packed, the vernissage. I accepted a plastic glass of champagne that turned out to be Guaraná soda—ultrasweet, the color of urine. I didn't know what the secret was to getting actual champagne. I had a look at the price list. Washington was making some real money.

A woman was talking to me. For some reason she assumed I spoke good Portuguese. I didn't correct her and my silence must have signaled comprehension. I was smiling, surely. Her facial expressions indicated that she was friendly, and I wanted her to like me, to continue speaking. She probably said her name, who she was, whom she knew, and in the fog of language panic I missed everything.

It turned out that she owned the gallery. "I like the art very much," I said in Portuguese, giving myself away. She switched promptly to English.

Because I spoke English it was assumed I had money and was a prospective buyer. The gallerist introduced me to Washington, the artist. He was born in one of São Paulo's most famous favelas, a place called Paraisópolis—Paradise City; his gallery knew how to make use of this background material. He didn't speak English, but for some reason I understood him more clearly than I had understood the gallerist. Perhaps he was speaking more carefully, for my benefit. Perhaps my brain was calming down. I finally had champagne. He, too, was under the impression that I was a prospective buyer, and I saw no reason not to play along.

My art says that poor people also want security. Poor people also want to protect what belongs to them. When we think of walls, we think of rich people putting up walls to keep out poor people. Dangerous people. But everybody wants to be safe. What if the Palestinians decided to build a wall? The Mexicans? My new work is inspired by a visit I made to Mozambique. I saw walls like this. I saw these walls around the homes of people who were upper-middle-class in Mozambique. But they were people who would be considered poor in Europe or America. I thought of my own city, São Paulo. I was thinking of the condominiums in Jardim Europa and Higienópolis, with those high, beautiful walls that look like Rome. I was thinking also of little walls, in Bixiga or Mooca, the little walls of my childhood. It is too easy to blame rich people for walls—everybody wants walls. It is what people do. Putting up a wall around your home is a kind of aspiration. It means you have something worth protecting. Even the poorest people have something they want to protect, something they purchased although they could not afford it. Poor people have doors and locks. You forget, most of the crime in this city doesn't happen to rich people. It happens to poor people. Poor people have smartphones, too.

Then he kissed me on the cheek and was gone. He held a glass but never took a sip. He knew how to work a room.

The gallerist, whose name I still didn't know, wanted to show me the back room. My husband joined us, and the conversation digressed into Portuguese. She wanted to show us more of Washington's work, but my eye was drawn immediately to some other framed prints, leaning against a wall. One struck me particularly. A field of scribbling that only after a moment's attention revealed itself as loops of crazed script. What language was it? Even if the text had been in English, I couldn't have deciphered it. It was writing that wasn't writing, a false calligraphy, unraveling as it fell to the bottom of the frame, words and letters tangled like steel wool. The gallerist saw my interest. "Ferrari," she said. The prints had come in the day before. "Do you know him? Do you know his work?"

I liked it. My husband liked it. We needed prices. We had no sense of the value, the going rate. She was going to say a number and we were going to decide if it was outrageous. The calculus had a certain purity. We were going to determine if the object was worth the price without the benefit of market knowledge. It struck me as incredible that we might buy a piece of art from a gallery and then take it home, as we would buy shoes we had just tried on; that anyone could do it. We could hear the rumble of the vernissage through the dark curtain that divided front from back. We were on the other side. We were buyers. The gallerist instructed an assistant to wrap the artwork in butcher paper.

We went out, into the night, the print under my husband's arm, swaddled in the brown, stiff paper. The print came in a good frame of blond wood. I had never owned art. It would hang on our wall and the only people who would be able to see it would be the people we invited into our home. This was art, privately held. I had seen the gallery labels in museums: *Private Collection.* My husband carried our collection under his arm. Anxiety struck me almost immediately. We were out in the night with something of real value.

We headed to a bar off Rua Harmonia with Iara and some of the others. Iara was delighted we had bought a piece. She couldn't stop talking about it. She and the gallerist and Washington, something, something. Marcos wasn't there; suddenly I couldn't remember if he had been at the gallery. The caipirinhas looked like drinks for children, festive and precious, aquariums of pure alcohol and colorful flotsam, kiwi and tangerine and pink peppercorns. There was a mural covering the long back wall, the city of São Paulo in black and white—the density of buildings, the avenues, the bridges, the parks. Iara was talking about a visit she had made to San Francisco. From the kitchen came the aroma of onions cooking in oil.

The younger people at the table were artists, the older ones Iara's friends. They all lived in Vila Madalena. Iara did not, but she had money and spent it on art, and so she was well-liked. Now we were people who spent money on art. Creativity had been sold. My husband took my hand under the table.

I knew he was tired. The Ferrari print was at my feet, ours. We had done that together. I was hungry and wanted to stay out. I thought I was understanding more than usual of the Portuguese being spoken around me; and I was perhaps also drunk. Everyone spoke excitedly of the protests, the manifestações. What would happen? How would it end? I was in love with my husband. The parks were empty. Rua Harmonia ran downhill to the cemetery.

After thirty generations, the average person will have more than a billion descendants.

León Ferrari's was a story of exile, a South American's story. He left Buenos Aires during the time of the generals there and came to São Paulo during the time of the generals here. The generals were crazy right-wing men, obsessed with anything vaguely radical. This was happening all over South America at the time, artists and intellectuals and rambunctious leftists wandering the political desert their continent had become, squirming away from one dictatorial regime and into the clutches of another, escaping arrest, waiting for news. Fernando Henrique Cardoso fled to Chile, Roberto Bolaño fled from Chile. León Ferrari lived in São Paulo for fifteen years and made art about crowds, traffic, highways. He drew Christian angels riding bareback on American-made fighter jets.

Hannah told me the news that Jean-Pierre had disappeared. Another man as well. By disappeared she meant the men had left the church's care without, to anyone's knowledge, acquiring work authorization or employment with one of the recruiters, and without telling anyone where they were going. They might have headed south, to the border with Uruguay, was one theory. Men on the move have a thing for borders.

Padre Piero was troubled by the possibility of criminal involvement. There were rumors of Haitians being drafted into the local gangs—running guns, transporting drugs. This seemed to me fearmongering, but I didn't really know. Padre Piero knew that even two Haitians mixed up in any of that would imperil all the rest of his work.

I could appreciate the attraction of disappearing. You boarded a train, which no one but you knew you were on, and you arrived in a city, which no one but you knew you were in, and you sat down at a café and ordered a sandwich and a beer, and a man brought you the sandwich and the beer as if nothing were the matter, and he took your money. The rest of the world would say you had disappeared, but you knew exactly where you were. You moved on without reporting your whereabouts. You didn't discuss decisions with anyone before you made them.

Two men from Haiti who were living in Brazil had disappeared. But they hadn't disappeared the way housewives disappear in Antonioni films or suburban children disappear in literary fiction. They were assumed to be alive, not dead; it was assumed they had made a decision. It could be said perhaps that they hadn't disappeared at all; or, if it could be said that they had disappeared, then they had disappeared long before—from Haiti, from their families, their people, their homes. Everything that had happened since, including the weeks they spent in the care of the church, was an event within this period of disappearance. Haiti was the only country they had known until a few months ago; and yet nobody thought they had returned to Haiti. Life there was already the past, the pluperfect.

"São Paulo has the world's largest population of crack addicts and the world's largest population of dogs under ten kilos."

"Have you been reading something?"

"It's palpable here. It's in the air. One side has so much more than the other side. You start seeing the signs everywhere. You could guess without being told that Brazil has one of the highest Gini coefficients in the world."

Every television screen in the building across from ours showed the soccer match. Fireworks detonated a few streets away.

"If you say things like that, you have to be able to explain what the Gini coefficient is."

"It's admitting that you can't have happiness without money. It's poor black kids robbing rich white guys who work for investment banks."

It was a dangerous line of thinking because if you took it too far everything beneath you started to crumble. Because it was only faith you were standing on. The faith that told you it was morally acceptable to live in this two-bedroom apartment, thirteen hundred square feet, and own these nice things, have a bank account and access to health care, potable water, etc.

Another night of protests. I watched on T.V. In Brasília, protestors climbed onto the roof of the Congress, and the camera lights below projected crazy alien shadows onto the white curved underside of the building's inverted cupola. The protestors were singing and chanting: a political invasion. Brasília was an organized city. The rigid streets, the rectangular lawns, the thin reflecting pools. A city that began life as a blueprint. Every square meter was planned out, a city dreamed up by a politician and his favorite architect; and now citizens were dancing on the lawns in front of government ministries. It was like a garden party filling up. There was a feeling of drunken abandon. Of possibility. This was happening in every city in Brazil. The people kept coming, they would not stop. Their demand—they had no single demand. The nation was in crisis. The systems of control that the politicians relied on were cracking apart. The World Cup was a year away and no one knew when the protests would come to an end. The elites looked fragile in their pleas for normalcy. Normalcy wasn't what people wanted, the status quo ante. The only word anyone could think of to describe what people wanted was *change*. Something had to change. The country, the politicians, the way things were. The course of events wasn't yet decided. I imagined the president in her palace, watching this from her window, not knowing what to do. A president is someone whose failure to meet expectations is almost ordained.

Iara called. She wanted to go, to be a part. I took a taxi to her building, and from there we continued to Avenida Paulista. My husband was at work; which is to say I didn't know where my husband was. I didn't leave a note.

Police stopped the taxi. The roads were closed. We overpaid the driver and walked the last kilometer on foot. The police looked tense.

Iara's older daughter had come with us. "I want my child to see this," Iara said. "We are making history. Brazil is making history."

People in masks were dancing; people singing and making music, more dancing. Horns and drums. It was a phantasmagoria of different meanings, mixed messages. A general drift of movement but no sense of hurry. More than anything the protest march reminded me of the street parades and block parties I had seen during Carnaval. White tungsten light from the office towers above—the banks, the foundations, the state industrial federation—rained down on the street, the people, spraying the heads of young Brazilians. During earlier protests the media made a fetish of counting those heads—one hundred thousand, two hundred thousand. An avenue of bodies, squeezed together, the image purpose-built for filmic consumption. And there they were, the cameras—

on tripods recording the scripted language of T.V. reporters, inside the smartphones in protestors' hands, mounted to the helicopters circling overhead. Police helicopters and news helicopters were indistinguishable in the dark. Was I considered a participant, now that I was inside this crowd of people? Was I counted? There must have been others who came only as witnesses. People watched videos on their smartphones of protestors in Brasília, protestors on Copacabana Beach in Rio de Janeiro, as surely people in Brasília and Rio were watching the footage from São Paulo; everyone was filming, posting, tweeting, sharing, hashtagging. They took selfies. They took crowd shots. A feedback loop, an ouroboros of self-reference, consuming and being consumed, the self-aware creation of spectacle: genuine political feeling became confused with the pleasure of common adventure, with festivity, the fear of missing out.

They would edit the footage later, they would choose the right filters.

They played bells, chimes, vuvuzelas.

I moved at the pace of the crowd.

I saw the elderly, and parents with small children. Iara was ecstatic.

I looked at the streets filled with people and thought of other consequences. Somebody was making money, somebody was losing money.

I usually have a skepticism of collective sentiment.

I saw skinny lone men with bare torsos and their shirts wrapped around their faces, covering everything but their eyes, chasing and being chased by the T.V. cameras. They would make the news because to the camera they looked like terrorists.

Luciano was somewhere in this crowd. I was looking for him, I realized—for a boy, disappearing himself in black clothes, some kind of mask, seeking purpose in anonymity and destruction. The foolishness of my attempt was obvious immediately, among waves of young men dressed in black, in masks, the torrents of people: you would never find anyone in this. He was there, and he wasn't there. Iara enthusiastically joined the group chants, beat the air with her fists.

She caught her breath. Her face, serious a moment ago, relaxed into a smile, then laughter. She was sweating. She pulled me into an embrace. "This is wonderful; I need some water," she said. Her face turned serious again. Her daughter was quiet, looking at the ground, away from everything around her.

Something was happening. I heard crackling, hissing. The *thunk* of metal landing heavily on stone. Yelling—but there was already yelling. The patterns of movement shifted, the direction. I heard the ordnance of megaphone voices. I saw a group of black-clad people advance toward the police line and throw something in unison, a payload of stones, or firecrackers, and then quickly retreat. Glass shattered nearby. More crackling, hissing. The pale gauze of smoke didn't dissipate—tear gas; the police were using tear gas. Something had happened. An hour had struck. For reasons I couldn't discern three policemen closed around a young man and brought him down with truncheons. The gas was getting in my eyes, a frantic rabid itching. The celebratory mood had vanished, replaced by something dark, medieval, unpredictable. In the confusion Iara and her daughter were missing; I'd lost them. Some people stood in place, others ran furiously. Some drifted like crowds after a match. More yelling, running. My eyes cooled. I walked and then jogged. They launched more tear gas, now at a distance from me.

I walked down from the avenue. Iara wasn't answering her phone. I passed lingering floes of people also leaving the protest. They radiated a nervous energy. I kept going. The shops were closed, the restaurants. There was nowhere to go inside. Nobody wanted his property damaged. Usually this neighborhood was lively, cosmopolitan; the shuttered faces of cafés made it seem desolate and abandoned. Some men passed me and I felt a gust of adrenaline. I thought of the boys who robbed us. They had not thought of me as often as I had thought of them, although perhaps I was wrong about that. I couldn't know. I passed another group of people who had come from the protest and saw a face I knew.

He wore a hooded sweatshirt. He came over when he saw me. He was trembling; he had been crying. He showed me his hands. There were cuts, blood. He began to cry again: Luciano seemed for the first time truly young, unformed. His body, vibrating, fell into mine, and I hugged him. "What happened? What happened to you?" I said. "O que passou?" He shook his head. He went on crying as I held him. In the air was a last remnant of smoke, and from somewhere nearby I heard the keening of sirens.

After a while he said, "You don't say anything?" "I don't say anything," I said. His friends were gone.

Later I learned that the police had used rubber bullets. Against the same crowd I was part of. So it was possible to have been there and not to have known. It was a crowd large enough to contain microclimates. There were reports of eye injuries. I watched the news with my husband, once he came home, and saw the footage of bloody faces under the lysergic strobe of police lights, camera lights. I watched again on T.V. events I had witnessed a few hours earlier. The barbaric yawp of the protestors could now be controlled with the volume button.

A gente vai abalar o Brasil!

I watched, and already it looked nothing like what I had seen.

"They want change. But what do they think change looks like? Change looks like other politicians."

"Why is it wrong for people to want change?"

"Because wanting change is vague. You don't get anything when all you want is change. Or else you get something you didn't expect," my husband said.

"They're sending the message that the status quo is unacceptable."

"I'm only saying that you have to know what you want."

"They know what they don't want."

"That's not the same thing."

"So what do you think happens with all this?"

"Nothing. Not much. I think it fades away. I think everything goes back to the way it was."

"I don't believe that's possible."

"I know you hate it when I put things in market terms, but when I look at these images on T.V., when I look at the hundreds of thousands of Brazilians in the streets, what I see is irrational exuberance. I see a phenomenon that cannot sustain itself."

"Do you realize this is the first time in forever we've argued about something other than children?"

"I didn't know this was an argument."

"Would you go to the protests if you were Brazilian?"

"I'm not Brazilian. This isn't my country. The protests aren't for me."

"What if I went?"

"Why would you go?"

Abalar—I looked it up. It means "to shake" or "to unsettle," "to upset," "to overwhelm." Of disputed origin, perhaps from Vulgar Latin, *advallare*: "to descend to the bottom of the valley."

DO YOU WANT SOMETHING?

Toll collectors on the highways leaving São Paulo made you wait after you paid the equivalent of ninety cents to receive a printed receipt of payment. This was to discourage theft on their part. On the back of each receipt was the name and picture of a missing child; as we drove, missing children accumulated in the cup holder. I looked at the slips of paper. Some of the children had been missing for so many years they were no longer children.

Marcos was driving. My husband was in the passenger's seat, and I sat in the back with Iara. We were going to a place called Paraty, a place by the ocean.

It wasn't supposed to be us, my husband and me. Other friends of theirs canceled at the last minute, and the reservation at the pousada was nonrefundable; at least this was the story Iara told me the night before. Our interest was piqued. We said yes. Paraty: an old colonial port, planted on some tattered coastline at the southern wedge of Rio de Janeiro State.

The name conjured a vision of Portuguese sailors, houses made of stone, the tall masts of ships. Gold going out, slaves coming in.

Marcos and my husband talked business in the front seat. The only names I recognized were the names of banks and companies; when they used a person's name it meant nothing to me. For my benefit Iara was counting the ways in which her parents were going to spoil her daughters while she and Marcos were gone.

We turned off the highway, the clean, inland speed of it, and drove down a tumbling, curling, almost impossible road; on the G.P.S. device Marcos was using, it looked ridiculous, more like a diagram of an intestine than something an automobile might navigate. It was not only curving but steep. The road was taking us down to the ocean. Marcos drove aggressively, a style of driving I'd come to associate with Brazilians generally, as he took every opportunity, including opportunities he should not have taken, to pass the cars ahead. Something inside me twisted sympathetically every time he slammed through another 180-degree switchback. From my seat, behind my husband, I could see Marcos in profile—round, shaven, darkish Southern European skin—and I wondered how he would react if someone actually managed to overtake him.

"They will buy them new dresses, they may buy them another dog, you never know," Iara said.

We continued shedding altitude, and then we were at the bottom, driving again on straight, flat asphalt. The Atlantic forest draped the hillsides in fronds and vines, waves of tropical density—nectandras, jacarandas, brazilwoods, pink jequitibá. On the passenger's side, the shelf of land fell away, depositing into ocean; mist lifted from the face of the ocean and flooded the air around us. My husband passed the digital camera back to me and said I was in charge of taking pictures.

On the G.P.S. map our dot was less than fifty kilometers from Paraty when traffic on the two-lane highway suddenly came to a halt. It had been stopped awhile; people stood outside their cars. Marcos left to investigate and walked up the road until he was out of sight. Farther on, I saw a nimbus of red and blue, the queasy pulsing of emergency lights. Marcos returned. "An accident," he said.

He and Iara spoke in Portuguese. A man was dead. When traffic at last started to move, I saw for myself. He was middle-aged and still lay in the place of dying. The body was in an awkward half twist, wearing jeans and a mustard-yellow tee shirt, and it had a strange, crumpled heaviness, a lurid animal weight, the limbs arranged badly, nothing like the body of a man asleep.

I saw the driver. He stood next to his car. No one spoke to him. He stared blankly, away from the body.

I imagined his mind, not racing, but empty.

We drove on, gained speed.

Marcos and Iara, in conversation between the front of the car and the back, speculated about how it happened, the angle of incident, based on where and how the body lay. My husband was silent, a silence I interpreted as shock, if only because I was in shock myself. Marcos and Iara seemed to consider it a routine matter. There was some cultural gap at work. We rode the gentle curves of highway above the photogenic green coves of Rio de Janeiro's coastline, the windy plains of water and jutting blades of beach. I tried to enjoy what I was seeing. I may have taken more pictures with the camera that was still in my hands. But the memory of the man's body, lying in the same rich yellow sunlight that glazed the beaches, was more vivid than a photograph. It wouldn't leave me, and I couldn't help but feel—as Marcos was again driving relentlessly and overtaking every car in our path—that we, too, should bear some guilt for the man's death.

That evening the four of us sat outside at the pousada with drinks, by the pool, the scene burnished perfectly by torchlight. We watched other guests walk through the garden among the palms and hanging lobster claws.

"I didn't expect it to be so crowded," Marcos said. "It's the middle of winter."

The next morning Marcos and Iara said they were going for a walk in town. We didn't see them again until nightfall. I don't know why this surprised me. We were two pairs of adults; we hadn't made an arrangement to spend the entire weekend together. My husband was slow to mobilize. I went to the front desk and asked what one was supposed to do in Paraty. They gave me pamphlets with pictures of speedboats and faux pirate ships. I made arrangements for a harbor tour.

At the pier were dozens of boats. Men called from the prows to anyone who walked past, picking off the tourists who hadn't booked ahead, while party music detonated from onboard speakers; in the smaller boats people lay on brocaded pillows like sultans. The bars on deck were already doing business. We found our boat—the *Netuno*—and lay on white vinyl daybeds fixed to the main deck, out of the sun. Engines rumbled impatiently in the water below. The boat rocked softly and knocked against other boats.

We sailed from shore. The deck hands brought plates of fried fish, chicken legs, cold Heinekens, caipirinhas, bottled water, fruit, white pudding. The boat maintained a low speed. The sun was strong, in spite of the season. When the boat stopped near a small island, in a traffic jam of other boats, our fellow passengers hurled themselves off the side and into the turquoise water. Swimmers helped themselves from a nest of foam water noodles on deck, and soon the water was a churning broth of bodies and colored foam noodles. No one swam far; and so the swimmers stayed stuck together in a single, glutinous horde. It was a spectacle whose absurdity was lost on the participants. At the next stop my husband and I jumped in. I worried about getting too much sun. I tried to move away from the horde, to put two meters of water around me in every direction, and I felt calmer. I peed in the ocean instead of using the bathroom belowdecks, which I assumed was disgusting. I was alienated, totally, from the people doing the same thing I was doing, certain their context was not my context. My husband found me in the water and kissed me, our feet batting together, and he put his hands on my legs, my breasts. Everything was stupidly pretty. Behind him was the coast of a small island, a narrow belt of sand tight around the jungle. I saw birds of unusual colors. All the Brazilians seemed to have waterproof cameras.

Back on ship, a man who overheard us speaking English

asked in English where we were from, and my husband responded in Portuguese, and of course the guy worked for a bank in São Paulo, and they talked about that.

At the next stop for swimming the man who was speaking to my husband held aloft one of his children and offered him up as a floatation device if all the water noodles were taken. The joke was a hit with the people nearby; and the child he was holding gave a peal of anguished delight.

My eyes were closed. I lay on the white vinyl daybed just out of the sun and enjoyed the delicious sensation of the ocean shrinking to salt on my skin.

That afternoon we learned why the city was so crowded. There was an international literary festival taking place, a semi-famous one, apparently. Writers had come from England, India, the United States, the Middle East, the Balkans. They had descended on Paraty to give readings and participate in roundtables, and they trailed an exhaust cloud of publishers, editors, hangers-on, in-the-know festivalgoers.

It was an editor back at the pousada who told us this. The editor was Italian, he had lived in Brazil for many years. He worked at the Companhia das Letras. It was a venerable house, he said; perhaps we knew the name. Three of his writers were to appear during the festival. There was a detachment of children playing in the pool while we talked, some mean-spirited game with a ball. The editor drank Campari over ice with a wedge of lime. His wife appeared, a Brazilian—sunned, freckled skin, at least a quarter century younger. The editor wore no shirt. He was the kind of older man who took care to delay his own decline.

The editor talked about his work. I was interested. His English was flawless. He was amused that we had come to Paraty without knowing about the literary festival, as if we were tourists in Rio who had come without realizing it was Carnaval.

"The real difficulty is getting our writers into translation. Among writers in Portuguese, you can tell me José Saramago, Clarice Lispector, and who else?"

I could tell him no one else.

"There you have it. You cannot name anyone, and you live here, you are a reader. Machado de Assis is the greatest Brazilian writer, and yet he has no following outside this country. Jorge Amado is another. I have an author, Bernardo Carvalho, he is a very significant figure in contemporary fiction. There is an excellent writer from Mozambique, Mia Couto. In Italy, we don't have any problem selling our writers abroad, but in Brazil, a country three times the size, it is much more difficult. Of course, you know, Brazilians will read Philip Roth or Ian McEwan in translation before they read their own writers. They will read Stephen King. We are always looking to America."

At some point, while the editor was talking, my husband stepped away, and I saw him now at the bar, chatting with a man there. The children were out of the pool; the pool was empty except for the ball they left behind, floating pointlessly from one end to the other on some invisible current. Everything had become still, picturelike. I saw this picture reflected in the editor's sunglasses, the tanning oil on his chest, the yellowing radiator of the lime wedge in his Campari.

"I should write down those names," I said.

The editor's wife moved in her chair, turning a different side up, though the sun was all but gone.

"My wife, Monica," he said.

Eventually Marcos and Iara surfaced. They were hungry. The streets were lively. Every hotel in the city was packed. The literary festival was in full swing. People met in the streets and embraced, everybody knew everybody. I had the feeling of arriving at a gathering in the home of someone I didn't know. By now I'd heard of three different events taking place just that evening, but the crowds they attracted didn't dent the crowds at the restaurants, all of which were idiotically full, as we found, going from one to the next, the four of us like a wandering troupe, hesitating at any remotely plausible option as we audited the menu and judged the ambience, there being a good deal of socially normal but situationally counterproductive politeness in all this as we tried to determine without directly asking whether any member of our party wished to veto an option. My feet were beginning to scream from all the walking on broken stones, when Iara remembered that there was a French crêperie, well spoken of, not indecently out of the way. We headed there and found that of course the crêperie was overrun as well. Marcos rounded up the owner, and whatever he said had an effect, because one of the two waitresses on duty produced a folding table and some chairs (which a moment ago they claimed not to have) and staged them on the sidewalk, out past all the other folding tables and chairs, almost a full block from the entrance to the restaurant, so far from its light that we were in near total darkness. The night was tropically hot in spite of the season. The waitress brought candles and carafes of warm red wine. It was the only restaurant on the street, the only real activity. After the drama of finding the restaurant, and then procuring the table, no one was in the mood for conversation. Iara lit cigarettes. Marcos and my husband fell back to the safe territory of work; they could talk about work all night if they had to. But soon Marcos and Iara got started: Brazilians possess inexhaustible reservoirs of talk. Fine by me, fine by my husband—we let them do the conversational heavy lifting. I had to kill a few yawns. Dogs roamed the darkness, just beyond our outpost, a sound of paws on the dirty, soft stones. They stayed along the edges of stone walls, walls that hid any view of the ocean, although you could sense a faint, briny presence, the nearness of water.

Iara said, "You know our friends, the couple that was supposed to come with us this weekend?"

She made a motion of breaking a branch in two.

"That is why they do not come."

"It was sudden," Marcos said.

The next day my husband was bored, and went for a walk in town. I opted to stay by the pool. I felt pleasurably stagnant, and ordered another drink from the barman. I was watching a Brazilian family, three people, and trying to puzzle out the relationships. My guess was father, adult son, and youngish stepmother, but Brazilian habits of physical contact made it difficult to decipher, and I kept changing my mind. The three of them stood chest deep in the pool, for hours, talking and drinking nonstop; they seemed not to notice when children invaded the pool and initiated a warlike sequence of messy dives. Then the editor's young wife came out to lie in the sun.

She had a truly excellent body, which she did as little to conceal as possible. I saw golden curls, like eyelashes, on her thighs; Brazilian women shaved down from the knee only. She lay on her stomach and aimed her face in my direction: with sunglasses on, she could have been watching me or not. I turned away. My husband came back. I didn't see if he looked at her. She shifted position as he sat down beside me.

"What did you find?" I said.

"I found a beach town. Kitschy little art studios where you wouldn't want to buy anything. A truly gratuitous number of ice cream parlors."

I was convinced the woman was looking at us again—at me or my husband, I wasn't sure.

"Bom dia," I said, and smiled. She made no response.

Then her husband was there, waving to us. He lay down and shut his eyes.

His wife reached over and touched the bony knob of his hip, briefly, before withdrawing her hand. It might have been routine affection, or a failed signal for attention. When he stirred a moment later, it was to reach for his book. His wife said something in Portuguese or perhaps Italian that I could hear but not understand. We were all of us in close proximity by the pool; no conversation was truly private. He looked at me, or seemed to, and then said something to his wife, sotto voce.

I felt a budding awkwardness, the kind that is perhaps unique to Americans.

I said, "Do you have no event to attend today?"

He smiled. "This morning, there was a talk, on the face of Islam in literature today. It was so dull, and so overheated with opinion, that I am now too exhausted to do anything more than this. My own writer makes his appearance tonight. I will feel much improved by then."

He lowered his eyes to his book. His wife rotated her head so that the silver mirrors of her sunglasses faced me once more, and lay that way for a long time. I tried to ignore what I felt sure was her stare. I couldn't know. Maybe she found my husband handsome—he *was* handsome, and his skin was newly tanned from hours in the sun. For a moment I looked at him like an object, a photograph, like something in a magazine ad: my husband as luxury good. He was reading the *Economist*. I wanted to point out the wife to him, the wife's behavior, but there was no way to do it without her noticing.

One possible reason for her interest was envy. I imagined how we looked in her eyes. My husband was roughly my age; he and I would age in the same way, at the same rate. We were comparably attractive. In ten years, perhaps not even that, the evidence of her husband's age would be ungovernable. Even now it must have cost him effort to maintain the engines of virility; it must have been difficult to be married to a younger wife sometimes. She must have thought often of death. But perhaps she was happy, perfectly happy, with her older husband, who surely gave her things a younger husband wouldn't. And her husband would never see her old. He wouldn't be there to see the decline of her beauty. He wouldn't ask her for children, presumably. She would have to care for a dying man, but she would be in the prime of life; she would have the strength for that kind of work. It would be a death she was prepared for. When my husband died, I would be dying, too.

She stood. I couldn't help feeling that she wanted to brandish her body for our attention. I sensed my husband turn his head slightly. Her act seemed to say: I could have had a man my age, but this was the man I wanted. She bent, slowly, and kissed her husband before going into their room. He said something to her. The kiss changed the feeling of the moment. He was so much older, his body so much further along the line of decay; her body was like a comment on his. What was sex like for them? Sex was important. What was it like to be a couple whose tenderness looked ridiculous? She was gone.

Some birds took off from a nearby tree, and for an instant they seemed to be falling, tumbling from the branch, before their wings inevitably gained traction on the air and they began to rise in staccato upward spurts. Their feathers were a bright, candyish shade of green I had never seen on a living thing. South America was filled with life that to a North American looked alien. The pool was briefly calm until the children returned. One by one they broke the surface. I waved over the barman to order another drink. My husband was asleep.

I heard a door open somewhere behind me. The wife. She

sat next to me. I looked over at the husband, but he wasn't watching. She was holding a book.

"My husband asked me to give you this. It is the book by his writer, the one who will read tonight. My husband thinks you will enjoy it. He says you are a lovely young couple. I can see that he thinks you in particular are lovely."

She said all this in crisp English, as if it were a speech she had rehearsed.

The wife returned to her husband. They lay awhile in silence and then went back to their room. He waved good-bye; she didn't. I wondered if I'd imagined this strange interlude, until I saw again the book she had given me, a novel in Portuguese whose title was a single word, which I didn't know. The gift of the book was an invitation: to attend the reading that evening; and perhaps to meet for something else, later. He made his wife the messenger. I didn't feel disgusted; I didn't feel anything about it. I knew already I wouldn't go. My husband was awake.

He didn't say anything to me. He jumped in the pool and swam aggressively for a dozen laps. He paused and then swam awhile longer. The pool was short and every few strokes he was forced to make the turn again. His body was beautiful, pulsing through water. When he finally came out, he was breathing hard, dripping, and he flagged down the barman before reaching for his towel.

"Do you want something?" he said to me.

"I'm having Campari," I said.

By the time the drinks came, his skin was dry again.

"I think Marcos and Iara are having problems," he said.

"Oh," I said.

"He talks a lot about the secretaries at work. All the men do, of course."

"But he doesn't confide in you."

"When Brazilian men sleep around, there's nothing to confess, it's a fact of life. Maybe he confides in a priest."

I said, "Iara and Marcos never mention church. I'm sure they baptized their daughters. I'm sure they assume we go to church, too."

"That's why they never mention it."

IN DEFENSE OF THIS LIFE

Las Vegas: money, golf, desert, kitsch, personal injury attorneys, hard bodies, sagging bodies, precancerous tans, smoking indoors. It is a place for people who want something, not for people who have something.

His parents, Hal and Gussie. His brothers, Mark and David. And their wives. Everyone is here. There are children.

There is going to be a party, friends of his parents not invited to the wedding in New York—our wedding, in three weeks' time, the decisions final. Hal and Gussie moved here recently, from Los Angeles, after Hal's retirement. It is the valedictory stage of life.

They live in a gated community: a closed society under a dome of perfect weather. The airport is nearby, chalky contrails across blue sky, shark's-teeth mountains in the distance.

Houses sit on the rim of a golf course, Hal and Gussie's edged against the fairway on the sixth. Spanish roofs of terra cotta, stucco walls. Retirees and Japanese women start golfing early in the day. A man in a pink shirt hollers about something that hasn't gone his way.

I enjoy the company of his parents, his brothers. Hal and Gussie aren't like my parents—they are talkative, instinctively warm, thoughtless with affection. Mark and David and their families live on the West Coast, Seattle and San Francisco. Their wives are from Idaho and Arizona. He is the only one in the family who moved east, and it makes him exotic. His brothers speak of New York the way they might speak of Paris: fondly, from a distance, a foreign city both charming and unusual in its ways. The West: mountains, rivers, the ocean.

Morbid heat, a high wind—the desert alternates between stillness and violence. I wonder about the feats of engineering required to maintain a healthy golf course here. I look at my watch, thinking I last checked the time thirty or forty minutes ago, and see that only ten minutes have gone by. This happens again and again.

We have lunch at the clubhouse, and Gussie introduces everyone at the table to the waitress by name and relation. Son, wife, son, wife, son, fiancée.

The work Hal retired from was similar to his son's. He misses it; it was a way of life. Now Hal does some day-trading on his computer. Father and son talk money, the fate of industry, the future. He is the youngest of his brothers. They are an oncologist and an environmental lawyer. They have other concerns. He isn't the one his father thought would follow him into finance, and so is a kind of disappointment. This is a thing I know without being told.

But Hal is a warm man, Gussie a warm woman. They overflow with parental qualities, grandparental qualities. I am embraced often, pulled in. The children are doted on: new members of the tribe. Hal and Gussie plainly enjoy the surround of family. Mark and David are unrelenting conversationalists, and their wives talk even more freely. They are polished women: they each have twenty perfect nails. They could be sisters. Both couples, in fact, are the kind that look like siblings. I've always found that sort of thing eerie.

Twelve people, three generations. I think of my own family, the quiet there, New England. The hard, calm molecule of a one-child family, where emotions have only three paths to take.

Eventually everyone scatters—the children to play, the parents to watch T.V., the grandparents to fall asleep.

It is easy here to slip into a lull. I lie on a lounge chair by the backyard pool, not reading the book open in my lap. Ahead of me is the pastoral of the golf course. Every few minutes I hear the dull *whumpf* of a ball erupting from the tee. Occasionally the sound of cursing, the gulp of a ball landing in water. Trees ostensibly protect Hal and Gussie's house, but it seems like only a matter of time before one of the solid white balls comes flying into the yard, crashing into the windows. A bad hook off the tee would do it. Birds animate the trees. I see robins, hummingbirds, ravens. They flirt, thrash. Golf carts migrate past at regular intervals, buzzing like lawnmowers. I watch through sunglasses. The blue of pools, blue of sky, the green of grass. The hostility of the desert is managed.

Dusk. We are gathered around the yard. The adults have drinks, babies loll in mothers' arms. The three-year-old always wants something; the two-year-old has begun to investigate the world on her own and needs constant monitoring. It is easy in this gentle chaos of family to speak or not to.

A jangle of family talk in warm darkness. They all have an extroverted ease with one another. Mark and David have an instinct for calibrating potentially offensive humor so that it doesn't offend. They're charming, in other words. The things they say, if I were to say them, would sound reprehensible. And of course men are allowed to say things women aren't.

Even these men, otherwise so confident, seek the affirmation of women. "I really didn't deserve that," David says, speaking of something at work, and then looks at his wife. The cliché of insecurity is a teenage girl; but it's not teenage girls who are insecure: it is men. I pick up other cues as his brothers look for a word from their wives, a glance, reassurance they are still on solid ground. And the wives never fail to give it.

We all turn at the sudden startled-animal sound of a ball skittering up the embankment and rattling against the fence rails. The wives gasp. Gussie hoots. Close one, Hal says. Hal's silver hair belongs on a yacht. Hal: *hale*.

He doesn't know why they moved here, his parents, why they left California. His brothers also find it mysterious—to move away from the ocean rather than toward it. No one asks the question directly. They seem happy. The decision was made between Hal and Gussie, a private matter, not a family one, and the children were informed only when the house in L.A. was sold and packed up, the keys relinquished.

The three brothers together give the impression of family conspiracy; although perhaps this is in my head, only a general unfamiliarity with siblings. He seems both like them and not like them.

I see strange things on the golf course. For one, people in golf carts drive much faster than seems wise. Two drivers shout and accelerate past one another; it isn't clear from a distance if this is bonhomie or anger. Given the nature of golf and the people who play it, mindless rage does not seem out of the question. The carts stop on the green, and the men step out, laughing among themselves, drinking beer and selecting putters. One of them performs a kind of dance, jackhammering his feet on the ground. More laughter. What have I witnessed? I feel like Lévi-Strauss, embedded among the natives of the Upper Amazon.

He steps outside to join me. I ask if he saw what I saw. I recapitulate the chase. Ridiculous, he says, but he doesn't seem especially amused. I suppose golf course behavior isn't as novel to him. He has golfed all his life. Hal first took him when he was five years old.

In defense of this life, he says, it's supposed to be a reward. It's supposed to come only after you've done something. After you've completed other pursuits.

My family likes you, he says. Really. And they know how I feel about you.

They're just so different from my family, I say.

Lunch at the clubhouse with the brothers' wives. This was someone's idea, I'm not even sure whose, and so it is just the three of us, the "girls"—when adult women are grouped together they are girls. The girls insist on rosé. I don't necessarily think this is a bad idea. Between them they have four children, ages one, one, two, and three. Among people with children, conversation has a way of shrinking rapidly to the common experience of parenting. Before I realize what is happening, we are deep into the indignities of pregnancy and motherhood, no holds barred: the often humiliating circumstances of one's water breaking, the horror movie of labor and delivery, a detailed toxicology report of infant excreta, an anatomy of the hazards a woman's body endures in the early months and years of a child's life. We go into some detail about the strange feast of breast milk, the rigorous schedules of pumping, the cracked nipples, the ineradicable smell of milk in clothes. I'm told of the mountainous boredom, of the deleterious effects of "pregnancy brain": apparently even a woman's intelligence has to suffer. There is a lot of laughter. I have the sense of being subjected to a kind of rite. At some point I open my purse to confirm that I took my birth control pill this morning.

Afternoon. A golf ball climbs the embankment, shoots through the fence, enters the yard. It comes to a stop. We all look at it, first in silence, then with laughter. A bit of excitement. Two in two days, Hal says, that's never happened.

The party is Saturday night, the day after tomorrow. We are calling it an engagement party. We were engaged months ago, but we can't call it a wedding party, since we aren't married yet. Saturday also happens to be the Fourth of July. Hal makes a joke about the irony of having an engagement party on Independence Day. All around the gated community I notice extra helpings of red, white, and blue.

We return to the clubhouse for dinner; bottles of wine are half-price. We talk about the wedding plans. There are details I find especially pleasing—an arts space in Brooklyn, music by a string band that plays rustic bluegrass—and feel like they belong to me even as I am aware of how many other people have similar tastes; but these things are somewhat arcane to his family. There was never a thought of using a church. I feel closer to him, perceiving how he is distinct from the rest of his family. Then I'm worried that we are talking about decisions already made in a way that reopens them for discussion.

Hal makes a remark about what good-looking children we're going to have. Just don't let them grow up to be golfers, he says.

Normally this is something I would let go without reply. He is only being kind. He is the father of the groom. It is the sort of thing he is supposed to say. But because of the wine, or perhaps some sediment of emotion building up during the visit, I say what I am thinking aloud.

Children aren't a given for me, I say. I've never seen myself as a mother, I say. I'm not one of those women who marry and end up erased, I say.

This causes a silence, the first silence I can remember since the visit began. The brothers, wives, parents. The children recognize it: they are precision instruments for sensing adult emotions. I can't say why I did it—perhaps I wanted to be a surprise again to this man who offered to marry me. Or perhaps I am only affirming something to myself by saying it aloud. I look away from everyone; I am not looking at him.

His family is my family now: this is a thing they have said to me repeatedly.

Well, Gussie says. Let's remember, all this is still a long way off.

Everyone stares out the tall windows of the clubhouse, at the dark course, the swells and traps.

I am not sleeping well here; but he appears to be sleeping normally.

Father and sons head out golfing. Conditions are ideal: clear sky, the wind docile. The brothers' wives go shopping; I decline. I'm alone with Gussie. She suggests I relax by the pool. With that book you've been reading, she says.

We're in the kitchen later, making lunch, when we hear a crash. We both know without turning. The window has a double pane; the inner glass was spared, but the outer is gashed through. Gussie and I go outside for a closer inspection, and a moment later a golf cart drives up, fast. It halts abruptly by the backyard fence. Two men. The one who steps out wears a hat with *Callaway* written across it. He stares for a moment at the broken window, assessing, expressionless. He doesn't speak. He takes out a checkbook and pen from a side pocket of his golf bag. This man signs a check, leaves the rest blank, hands it to Gussie through the fence. Then he and his friend drive off, the matter settled, apparently.

Gussie opens a bottle of chardonnay. We scrub tomatoes and cucumbers for a salad. Gussie spelunks in the refrigerator for more provisions. You're a bit different from my other sons' wives, she says, handing me more tomatoes.

I don't mean it in a negative way.

She says, I didn't feel right telling the boys why we left California. I don't want them to think badly of their father.

The chardonnay glows in a beam of sunlight just as it would in an advertisement.

I knew about it, she says. Something got into Hal, something about retirement, the way men are. But then it spread around, it was just embarrassing. Hal ended it, I believe him that he ended it, but I just couldn't stay in the same city. All three of us there like that. I couldn't stand the idea. I didn't make him beg, nothing dramatic. Just the one condition. Leaving. I had to leave. I had to make a fresh start. That was my condition.

Water spills from the tap through my hands. I turn it off and set the tomato down to dry. I don't know if I'm supposed to talk.

I ask, Why Las Vegas?

Gussie laughs. She says, Why not Las Vegas?

I wouldn't have imagined it of Hal. That is the point, of course; that is her point. No one would have imagined it. He is a man of almost overbearing affection, to Gussie most of all. The point is: *Even a good man.*

What I want to tell you, Gussie says, is that you will surprise yourself with what you feel later on. You don't know. That's one of the things marriage does to you.

And then it's the day of the party. The guests are Hal and Gussie's neighbors in the community, acquaintances from the club. They are strangers to us, and really they are strangers even to Hal and Gussie, people they have met once or twice. Only a few people come in from L.A.

We are congratulated. I am congratulated. It is the only thing people have to say to me. My accomplishment is marriage, the promise of marriage. I take questions about the venue, the food, the dress, the hair, the honeymoon. No one asks how we met. Everyone has advice, predictions.

You are going to look gorgeous in that dress, a woman says to me. She is the nth wife of a retired financier. Her teeth are like Formica.

You are going to have such a beautiful wedding, she says. She is like an oracle: she is so confident of what I am going to have.

No one asks what I do. It is assumed that what I do is marry.

One of the brothers' wives catches me. She says how wonderful the party is, the crowd. She is so kind. His family is so kind. You're glowing, she says.

I say, Isn't it pregnant women who glow?

Every time I look up, no matter where I am standing, he is on the opposite side of the yard. But I am never without company; I am always in a group of three or four. Strangers hug me—everyone hugs me. I am common property; fair game. Meeting so many unfamiliar people at once gives me an unsettled feeling, a sense of being out of place. In New York, we share the same friends, the same social world. I know his people, he knows mine. Here, in a city I'm visiting for the first time, buffeted by strangers, I feel like a woman entering an arranged marriage, not marrying for love, not marrying a man I know well, whose life is already my life. Someone new approaches, arms out. The bride, he says.

The fireworks begin just after dark. Everyone looks up, toward the Strip. Explosions bloom over the desert, neon palm trees, glazing the white skin of faces in a pink and green light. I feel the concussions in the bottom of my throat. Even miles away I smell sulfur and chemicals.

Independence Day. It is not a holiday I have strong emotions for. A nation's birthday seems as silly to me as a nation's feelings, a nation's relationship status. I catch sight of the three-year-old: he is enchanted. Holidays become meaningful or not during childhood. I have only a pleasant memory of summer nights, a field at dusk, the warm, gummy air.

While people are still distracted by the show, I slip away, into the house. It is cool, dark, silent. There is a back room they don't use, filled with boxes of stuff, forgotten things, photographs, old paperwork, school assignments—drawings, writing graded with stickers. Hal and Gussie dumped this stuff here when they arrived. Miscellaneous junk. Kid junk. It is a room out of mind. Some of the boxes aren't sealed. There is no organization. One of the first things I find is an essay he wrote in elementary school, printed in dot matrix, on the history of the machine gun: what ten-year-old child writes about the development of military technology? Would he even remember writing it? I set it aside. I continue searching.

I don't know how long I've been gone from the party. Who finds me? Gussie.

Hal wanted to throw it all away, but I couldn't, she says.

She picks up the essay her son wrote on the history of the machine gun; she turns a page. She says, I remember this: he was fascinated by this. She laughs.

Boys, she says.

People in the yard are clapping: the show is over. We return to the party. I lose Gussie in the crowd. She hugs me before going. I don't know what the hug means; but it is something beyond the affection she has shown me previously. She is not a stranger. She will become the member of his family I am most fond of. I will tell her things I don't tell my husband; I will tell her things about my husband. She will become more familiar to me and also more mysterious. But we won't speak again about what happened between her and Hal. I won't know fully the contours of her decision. I won't ask the question I want to ask her: *What was it like to give your life to your children?* I will always wonder about Hal, whether moving away from L.A. really closed the matter with the other woman. There is a kind of ease you can buy and a kind of ease you can't. I only know the future I know.

I find him outside, in the yard, and take his hand. I was just reading your latest thinking on machine guns, I say. In another town, farther out, fireworks are still exploding, a distant, vaporous glow over the desert. Later, the subject of children will come up again, and I will say, I don't know. It was something I felt strongly about when I was younger, I will say. We're still young, he will say, even though we will be older than we are now. Children are a decision society makes for you, I will say. He will say, Please don't use the phrase "capitalist imperative" when we're talking about this. We will have many conversations, over years, about this question. Some will be painful. I don't know this now. I don't know how young I am. I don't know what will change and what won't. I don't want this to be the only important thing, I will say. But it is an important thing, he will say. I say, will say, I love you.

PROTO-ROMANCE

Elizabeth Bishop, a person I admire, once lived in Brazil. She wrote a book about the country for the Life World Library. She fought with the publisher over points of style, and complained theatrically about it in letters to Robert Lowell. In the book, her affection for Brazil is plainly in evidence, as well as an eye for its excesses and injustices. "It seems that there should be a revolution every month or so," she wrote. You have to be an outsider, sometimes, to see things as they are. But you have to be the kind of outsider who drinks the liquor and sleeps with the locals. She lived there twenty years, more or less, and did both.

She personally knew Clarice Lispector. "I suppose we are getting to be 'friends,'" she wrote to Robert Lowell. "Her novels are NOT good." Writers. The life made of art, and all that.

"Oh, tourist," she wrote, in another context. By her own estimation, she spoke Portuguese "like a dog." Some comfort in that, I suppose.

Marcos started sending me texts. I failed to inform my husband of the texts, which at first didn't seem grievous; and then it did, and then Marcos suggested we meet. I asked what he had in mind. He wrote back: "Lunch, kisses." Brazilians often signed off with "beijos," but Marcos wrote the word in English. It altered the implication. He knew what he was doing.

Our rendezvous was set for an Italian restaurant, just off Avenida Faria Lima. Men in suits emerged from cars with the luxury items they were dating and handed the keys to valets, who ran here and there in sharp, practiced lines, like ball boys between points of a tennis match. I stepped inside and breathed cool, expensive air.

"This is where São Paulo businessmen bring their girlfriends," Marcos said between touching my hip and kissing my cheek. I saw a young woman with a man who was more than trivially older. "So this is where you can see them in the wild," I said. Marcos flicked his fingers in the direction of the waiter, and a moment later we had wine.

I could have said this was an English lesson over lunch. I didn't expect to be questioned, but it was good to have a way of explaining the situation, to myself, among others.

Trying to think of things I didn't know about him, I asked what Marcos's parents did for a living.

"They own property," he said.

"And Iara's?"

It seemed polite to acknowledge the fact of his wife.

"Supermarkets."

Marcos named an expensive chain where I bought French butter and almond milk. He dipped a piece of fresh bread into the dish of olive oil on the table between us. As he chewed, he made a face of uncomplicated pleasure.

I said, "Can you tell me what my husband does?"

"Do you mean with other women?"

I wasn't expecting that.

I said, "I mean actually what he does. His day. His job. I've never understood the nature of his work."

Marcos dipped his bread again. More pleasure.

I said, "People ask me what my husband does. I act as though it's inherently difficult to understand, that the fault isn't mine, but I'm not an idiot. I could understand it if I wanted to. The truth is, I've never bothered to learn about his work. I've never paid attention. I don't ask. The work he does—the work all of you do—bores me to death."

He laughed and clutched at his heart as if I had reached across the table and lanced him with my salad fork. He really was quite handsome. When he was finished with this performance, he leaned across the table so that his nose was almost touching mine.

He said, "So tell me something that does not bore you."

"Etymology," I said.

Success—a word he didn't know. It didn't seem like cheating; the word for *etymology* in Portuguese is a cognate. From the Latin: *cognatus*, "of common descent." He was unprepared for my style of flirtation.

Was I flirting? I wasn't not. You can call almost anything flirting, though, just like you can call almost anyone a friend.

Here's a tip, from my stint as a single woman in New York: if you're going to flirt with someone reading a book by herself, you'd better be ready to talk about the book. She'll be less than impressed if you ask her what she's reading and then stare like an idiot when she says Coetzee.

I saw another protest march on TV. It was on Avenida Paulista, the Museum of Art, a Sunday afternoon. The museum is an enormous, elevated concrete shoebox standing on red concrete stilts, whose primary architectural advantage is to give the titillating impression that one day it will collapse and kill everyone standing beneath it. The building was conceived by Lina Bo Bardi, Brazil's famous woman architect. Elizabeth Bishop's lover during her time in Brazil was also a woman architect, but she was famous more for being Elizabeth Bishop's lover than for being an architect. And for killing herself—pills, New York.

I wondered if Iara was at this protest. I had thought of calling her since having lunch with her husband, but always stopped myself. I didn't call because I didn't know what I would say. Telling her about Marcos seemed impossible, but speaking to her without telling her seemed impossible as well. Finally, I sent her a text message saying that I hoped her daughters were well, and she replied with a picture of the two of them dressed as princesses. I asked if she was going to the protest. There was a long delay before she responded. "What protest?" she wrote.

The protestors gathered under the Museum of Art and also in the avenue. Traffic was defeated in both directions. Already it was becoming corporate, co-opted; there were celebrities and local politicians on a dais, making speeches, polishing their brands. The police looked calm; they were getting the hang of it. So were the vendors. They sold vuvuzelas, Brazilian flags, tee shirts with slogans. The protestors were dressed in Brazilian national jerseys as if going to a soccer match. The vendors were dressed in jerseys, too, and they walked through the crowds, calling out what they had for sale, monetizing outrage. The weather was nice. I saw a sign in English: "Brazil is being raped by corruption." Signs in English? The intended audience wasn't Brazilian. The audience was CNN.

Change—after all this time no one had a better explanation for what the protestors wanted. But who doesn't want change? My husband was right: it's meaningless to demand only change. Everyone wants *x* but eventually finds herself wanting *y*, and then, before long, *z*.

"No one thinks it's going to go any further. The company's too big for this to become more serious than it has to be."

"So they were stealing."

"They were stealing so that they could pay bribes to politicians who would allow them to continue making money so that they could continue stealing and thus continue paying bribes."

"Is your bank going to lose money?"

"We have a position in the company. We're somewhat exposed. We're waiting on the outcome of the investigation."

"Right now it sounds like you're reading from your talking points."

"It's a global investment bank. We have talking points."

"You do?"

"Yes, we do."

"So tell me something that isn't a talking point."

"The politicians take bribes so they can finance election campaigns and remain in office so they can continue collecting bribes to finance more campaigns. The companies have internal divisions specifically devoted to processing the payment of bribes."

"No wonder people are protesting. The party in power is the party that does this?"

"Whatever party is in power is the party that does this. All the politicians from all the parties do this. When they're in power, they steal, and when they're out of power they open investigations."

People sent e-mails. They asked about Brazil, about my life in Brazil. Sometimes I answered. I wrote about restaurants, about the tasting menus and the wine pairings. I wrote about what I knew of the country's politics. The president's popularity was in free fall, the elections were a year away. The party depended on the poor for votes. People asked about the protests. They'd read stories in the *New York Times*. It was the only thing they knew about what was happening in Brazil. I wrote about traffic and crime. In one e-mail, I described an exhibition of photographs at the Museum of Contemporary Art. The photographer was a German Jew who had left Berlin in 1939 and landed in São Paulo. He became successful as a commercial photographer and made beautiful black-and-white images of industrial plants, Mercedes-Benz dealerships, adding machines. The exhibition included some of his early work. Before leaving Berlin, the photographer, when he knew he had no choice but to go into exile, took pictures of the lampposts and streetlights. This made perfect sense to me.

I saw the prostitute who lived in her car. I hadn't seen her in a while. I'm sick, she said. I offered her some money. I'm leaving here, I'm going home, she said. I asked where home was. I'm going home to die, she said.

My husband's hours at work grew even longer, and when he finally came home, the situation there lingered as a source of anxiety. I asked him about it. "Market conditions," he said. I asked what he meant. "I mean the way of doing business here," he said. "I'm tired," he said. "This fucking place," he said.

Hannah said, "Emmanuel came back from the American consulate this morning. He was so upset. 'They say I am not qualified!' He paid one hundred sixty dollars for a three-minute interview. He told the consular officer where he works, how long he's been in Brazil, how much money he makes, where his family is. And then he said he wanted to visit Disney for a week. Disney, because he knows that's what the Brazilians say. And I said, 'You're telling them you want to go for tourism, but you're obviously not a tourist, of course you didn't get a visa.' I realized that I sounded just like the consular officer. I felt awful. He said, 'So how am I supposed to go?' "

"He seemed to think the decision would be overturned if he could get *me* to say he was qualified for the visa. People always plead their case with you after the fact, even though you can't do anything about it. Everyone just wants somebody else to say he's right. Mackenson, Nadège, Frantz, Robenson, Cassandra, Wilguens, Mardochée—they all go to the consulate to be refused. The irony is that they have a better deal here than they would in America. They get papers here. They get health care. They must know it's hopeless. But they go anyway. They save up their hundred sixty dollars and they go. They can't even say *why* they want to go to America. They just want to go. Somehow they still believe in it, the myth, streets paved with gold."

"I get it. It's arbitrary that I was born in a rich country and they were born in a poor country. It's not fair. Americans don't try to sneak into Haiti. So I get it. Being at the bottom in America is a hundred times better than being at the bottom in Brazil, a thousand times better than being at the bottom in Haiti. I get it. But if you opened the borders, you would have literally half a billion people trying to get into the country. Is there a single person in Haiti who wouldn't come to America? These guys have a good situation in Brazil, and yet instead of making a life here, they're trying to get to America. Once upon a time I would have read about Haitian immigrants and I would have wanted to help them all. I would have been so angry at the politicians who want to keep everybody out. And now—but I get it. Fuck. I feel like that Republican senator who found out his son was gay and suddenly had to be O.K. with gay marriage."

Hannah would leave Brazil soon and return to Los Angeles. She had a dissertation to write and a C.V. to monetize. She had parents who wanted to see their daughter. We were in the church kitchen, where we often were when we talked about the men and women we helped, or tried to help. I had never seen Hannah like this. I thought of her as a young woman, though she was, in fact, a bit older than I.

"Do you think you'll ever have children?" I asked, surprising myself as much as I surprised Hannah by the question.

I read an article in the metro section about rising crime in the poor parts of the city. The article told the story of a couple in an outlying neighborhood who robbed the same pharmacy on three consecutive Sundays. They took diapers, formula, and the cash in the register. On the fourth Sunday they broke with the pattern and hit another pharmacy—but it was on the same street, and the man was shot dead by police.

We had plans for another trip. We had the tickets, reservations. Then my husband canceled at the last minute—work, what else. We were supposed to visit a preserved colonial city in the hills of central Brazil called Ouro Preto. Elizabeth Bishop once lived there; her house still stood. I was disappointed. I had wanted to see it. My husband said I should go on without him.

He was at the office already when I took a taxi to the airport. Navigating an airport solo, without my husband—it was the first time in years I had traveled alone. The airport was different without him. Airports force you into a set of tasks requiring concentration inside a cinema of distraction; and Brazil's airports were lousy with low-level criminal activity. Traveling with my husband, I could divide the required tasks, and in fact it was he who typically steered us through them. Now I was stepping toward the bag drop before I had my boarding pass. I wasn't following procedure. There were signs behind the counters about an airport tax that I'd never noticed before. I decided not to ask anyone about it. I could see that there was in our marriage something of a protector-protectee dynamic. There were aspects of the world that, because of my husband, I had the luxury of not paying attention to. It occurred to me that marriage is another thing you can describe as nonlinear.

"At least I know you aren't having an affair," my husband said, before I went away on my own, a joke.

When you study a foreign language, among the first words you learn are *mother*, *father*, *husband*, *wife*. They are the words that organize relations, unremarkable outside the context of your own life. But once I was married, two of these words, *wife* and *husband*, suddenly took on a new, strange vibrancy. I was somebody's wife. My husband was my husband. I felt something in my skin, even my heart—a feeling between elation and alarm—when I heard myself using these most basic terms, *husband* and *wife*, which seemed like things that did not belong to me.

Do you mean with other women? Marcos had said.

Flying for miles over the hard tundra of clouds that separated the plane from the world below. A storm. On descent, the turbulence grew fierce, and I was queasy, which was unusual for me, and unusually anxious; the state of the plane felt perilous. I tried to control my anxiety with a rehearsal of the basic physics that kept an airplane afloat on air, but I was unconvinced. I studied the flight attendants' faces, calm, even bored; but their performance of normalcy, as they wheeled the drinks cart down the aisle, didn't reassure me. From where had come this urgency to visit Elizabeth Bishop's house? I could have waited until my husband was free to join me; we could have changed the tickets. Instead, we had conspired to be apart for a few days. There was a dark thought I was trying to keep at bay as the airplane bucked and rumbled: I didn't want to die yet because my life was not the life I wanted. Rain lashed the windows all through the descent, and the wing, the city below.

The central square of Ouro Preto was a tilting floor of uneven cobblestones, endlessly circled by birds, under a sky of voluptuous gray. At the tourist office I found a huddle of men in army-green jackets. They had the air of a guild. I chose one who said he could speak English. As if I'd put a coin into a slot, he immediately started to tell me about the soot-black church in the square. Ouro Preto seemed like one of those places where not to hire a guide would be churlish. I said I wanted to see the house where Elizabeth Bishop had lived.

It had blue doors and brass fixtures. It sat on a narrow, bending road that ran lazily uphill from the main part of the city, and behind the house the land formed a valley of black and deep, hard-packed green, speckled with little red roofs and coal-black steeples. Elizabeth Bishop's house turned out to be a house, in other words. A modest bronze plaque identified it as the house where the American poet had lived for ten years. I took some pictures. I took a picture of the plaque.

The guide gave a lecture on Marxist themes disguised as a historic tour. As he told it, the government was little more than a clique of elites who produced a fraudulent, self-dealing version of history in the service of protecting their own interests, and he seemed to consider it his duty to give the other side of the story. I liked him. Another guide would have insisted on the Santa Claus version of history, assuming this was what tourists wanted. Instead he drew attention to failure, official hypocrisy, episodes of moral cowardice. He also told a lot of jokes. He saved them, it seemed, scavenged them, ready to deploy his jokes on Americans. He seemed to believe that Americans loved nothing more than a good joke. "The Pope comes to New York and the driver picks him up in a limo. But the Pope wants to drive, and so the driver sits in back, because in jokes everything is possible." He told jokes as we navigated the cramped streets; the streets of the city were lightly scented with liquor. I took my bearings by whether we were walking uphill or downhill; otherwise the corners seemed to repeat themselves. The guide moved decisively. He touched my elbow when he wanted to make a point or to steer me out of harm's way.

He took me to the Museum of the Inconfidência. It commemorated an eighteenth-century rebellion against the Portuguese crown inspired by America's revolution against England. The revolutionaries themselves were an odd bunch, not obviously destined for success, a grab bag of ex-soldiers and failed poets. They were manqués of all stripes. Their true goal wasn't Brazilian independence, but commercial autonomy for their mineral-rich state. Political leaders had tried to obscure this fact ever since, the guide said, in order to use the incident as a foundation stone in the national myth. In any case, the thing didn't come off. The revolutionaries were exiled to Africa, except the leader. He was called Tiradentes—Toothpuller. The Portuguese hanged him and quartered him. More than a century after the fact, the government got the idea of making Toothpuller a sort of Brazilian George Washington, and declared the date of his death—his martyrdom—a national holiday.

I ate lunch with the guide at a restaurant he recommended. It was a cafeteria, food sold by weight; not a place tourists came. I was skeptical until I tasted the food. He asked if I wanted a beer or a glass of wine, and I said wine, and then one of the boys loafing near the cash register brought it for me. We didn't talk much while we ate. I checked my phone and saw some texts from my husband, and a few from Marcos, all of which I ignored. "You have a boyfriend or something in America?" the guide asked. I slowly chewed a sun-dried tomato down to the skin. "Do you have a wife?" I said. "No, but I have kids," he said. He ate olives and pulled the pits from between his lips and arranged them in a row on the edge of his plate.

In the hollow belly of a church, the guide named the saints, wooden statues stationed in the eaves, and told me their stories. Anthony was the patron saint of lost things and unmarried women, and a magnet for superstition. An unmarried woman may bury Saint Anthony upside down until he brings her a husband, or else on the eve of Saint Anthony's feast she may fill her mouth with water and wait to swallow it until she hears somebody utter a man's name, which then she knows is the name of the man she will marry. The guide told me this and then waited for me to say something.

Under the baroque scowl of yet another church front was a market where boys and young women sold dishes made of soapstone and soapstone trinkets and soapstone replica churches. The stuff was piled in stalls like rubble, washed by rain, etched with birds and other animals. The soapstone sellers perched on low stools, working on the next thing, surrounded by all the unsold surplus already larding their tables, apparently undeterred by the extent to which supply outpaced demand. They picked at the soft material with pocketknives and thin files, giving the impression of deep concentration. It was work that could go on forever—refinements. This was our last stop, and the guide encouraged me to buy something, a memento. He was doing his part for the local economy; he wanted tourist money to go to the people who depended on tourist money. I chose a small replica church and the boy insisted on etching my name into the side. Emma—my mother's choice. A name with a lot of literary overhang, it has to be said.

In Brazil, there is a tree called the *mata-pau*—the killerwood. The name is well-deserved. The killerwood starts life parasitically, spawning and growing upon a healthy tree, its roots extending and thickening and strengthening, powerful tentacles that descend toward the soil; once the roots engage the ground, they begin poaching water and nutrients from the host tree. The killerwood strengthens its grip and finally strangles its host to death. It may encase the host tree like a skin. Once established, it lives like this, forever embracing the corpse of the tree it murdered. The killerwood is unique to South America, and even produces fruit—figs.

At the church, I found that Hannah was already gone. I saw Boaventura, and he didn't mention it. It seemed like an admission that he, unlike Hannah, would never leave. The ridiculous freedom of a U.S. passport, I wanted to say to him.

Elizabeth Bishop, in that volume for the Life World Library, wrote that in Brazil there should be a revolution every month or so. This was 1962. Then came the coup d'état, the long military dictatorship. She was supportive, on the evidence of her letters. So. She wrote to Robert Lowell: "But this *isn't* my world—or is it?"

Padre Piero pulled me aside. Something has happened, he said. Four of our Haitians were assaulted. They were returning to the church in the evening, from jobs they had just started, and were attacked by a group of men yelling *Africanos!* The men beat them and stole everything they had, phones, money. They were hospitalized. I didn't say anything as Padre Piero spoke. When he stopped talking, he put a hand on my shoulder, as if I were the one who needed comfort. Then I realized I had tears in my eyes. Oh, what a thing, what a thing, Padre Piero said.

Someone e-mailed me a map of Brazil that identified the states by their literal English translations. Green Water, Great Northern River, River of Crabs, Thick Bushes, Thick Bushes of the South. There was a Bad for Navigation, a General Mines. Rio de Janeiro, it's easy to forget after saying it a thousand times, is the River of January. The person who sent me the map did so because she was amused—what a funny country, being the point. There was a Place of Rain, a Holy Spirit, a Toucan's Beak. For the most part they were Indian names. You can play the same game in America. Illinois is the Land of Those Who Speak Normally.

"Do you remember?"

"We stayed at that bed-and-breakfast."

"We weren't married yet."

"The weekend in the country. The bed-and-breakfast."

"I remember being happy that weekend. The morning light in the woods. There was a brook. The rich air."

"We visited that house, the famous house."

"Fallingwater."

"Because you once had that poster on the wall in your dorm."

"I told you that. I wanted you to understand why it was important to me."

"Because you once lived with an image of a place you hadn't seen in real life. Because you didn't want a photograph to be a substitute for reality."

"It was so crowded with visitors."

"You hated that. You hadn't considered the inevitability of other tourists."

"I had the wrong idea. I imagined an empty house. I thought maybe there would be a gray-haired woman, a docent, to show us around."

"Now you don't have to go there at all. Now you can take a virtual tour on your phone."

"Is that true?"

"It must be."

"We bought that print in the gift shop, the small one, we framed it. Do we still have that?"

"I don't know. I don't know where it could have gone."

There were texts from Marcos. Sometimes I responded, sometimes I didn't.

Iara was my friend, the only friend I had made in São Paulo, really. I hadn't seen her in a while, not since I had lunch with Marcos. She suspected her husband of infidelity—she had made this clear without ever stating it directly. And now I had proof that she was right to suspect him. Did I suspect my husband of infidelity? I wasn't certain. I couldn't quite imagine it; and yet I knew that you should assume your own imagination has its fair share of blind spots.

Proto-romance refers to the last common ancestor of the modern Romance languages. It is an unknown tongue that nonetheless had to exist in order for Latin to become French and Portuguese and Italian. Something had to exist in between. It would have crept around the darkness of Europe, at the back end of the Roman empire, evolving, branching into new forms. Nothing of it was written down. It was a language of soldiers and slaves, something that survived by traveling. It is, in other words, the missing link—a theory, lacking a fossil record, but necessary to explain how we got from there to here.

Empires—there are always empires.

TEXTS

I was rereading *The Heart of the Matter*, disappointed to find that it didn't live up to my memory of its power from the first time I read it, in college, when my phone buzzed with a text from my husband. I read on a bit longer; failing to enjoy Greene as I did when I was younger felt like a betrayal of that younger self, that pre-husband, pre-everything self. I started skipping pages. I saw too easily the formula of plot. "It was like the hint of an explanation—too faint to be grasped." My memory of reading the book wasn't even ten years old. My husband sent another text.

He was texting to inform me that he had to stay late at work.

"No problem," I replied.

The phone buzzed again.

I assumed with a message intended to mollify me.

Except this time it was Marcos, not my husband.

"A question for my professor," he wrote.

I didn't respond to this, and in the time during which I didn't respond, my husband sent another text.

"Hope not too long," it said.

"You know what is my favorite word in English," Marcos wrote.

"It always takes longer than you think," I wrote to my husband.

"Moon," Marcos wrote.

"I wouldn't have thought," I wrote.

"You mean the word," Marcos wrote.

"Have a drink with Iara," my husband wrote.

"Or don't," my husband wrote.

"Or something else," Marcos wrote.

"I don't know," I wrote to Marcos and my husband.

"I am thinking of the word because I can see the moon from this window," Marcos wrote.

"Don't be upset," my husband wrote.

"My favorite word in Portuguese is either cidade or saudade," I wrote.

Marcos texted again. Except it wasn't Marcos, it was my husband.

"I'll be there as soon as I can."

"It's O.K.," I wrote to my husband.

"O period K period."

"I prefer it with the periods."

"I know."

"Go. Do your work."

"I am at the hospital."

"Why are you at the hospital? Should I come?" I wrote.

"My daughter," my husband wrote. "I am here because my daughter is sick. Yes. Come."

Of course my husband didn't write that, since we did not have a daughter, and of course I had written the last message to Marcos, not to my husband. It was Marcos who was at the hospital with his daughter.

"My wife is at home," Marcos texted, although that also would have been true if my husband had texted it.

"Here I go," my husband texted.

Text—the origin of the word concerns weaving, something woven from many threads.

"Hospital very cold and I forget to bring sueter," Marcos wrote.

I found two of my husband's old sweaters and took a taxi. Marcos was sitting in his daughter's room, in the only chair. He stood when I came in.

I gave him the sweaters, and he set them down.

"Your daughter," I said.

We looked at the girl in the bed.

He said, "It's her heart. The blood is coming out in the wrong places. A—vazamento."

He opened his hand, spreading his fingers, as if allowing water to fall through.

"A leak," I said.

"A leak," he said. "From birth. Congênito."

"Congenital," I said.

"Yes, congenital disease. She must have the surgery. For Juliana, five times now, like this."

"I didn't know."

"How would you know?"

Marcos closed his hand around his daughter's small foot, under the blanket.

"She is sleeping," he said.

She was indeed asleep, powerfully asleep. Her small body was full of strong drugs. She could have been in a coma.

"Let's go downstairs to the café," he said, and turned off the lights.

It could have been the café at a train station, an airport—hospital time like airport time, the hours of the day losing their fixed identities. Marcos bought two five-ounce bottles of merlot, like the bottles they serve on planes, and poured the wine into plastic cups. News played on a T.V. Doctors in white coats ordered espresso, preparing to stay awake for who knew how many more hours, laughing with each other, secure in the power of the knowledge they possessed.

"We never continued our English lessons," I said.

"Coração is heart. Filha is daughter. Mulher is woman, wife, it is both."

"That's a Portuguese lesson."

"I think she will be O.K.," he said after a moment.

"O.K.," I said.

"Yes—it is what her doctors tell me."

"I would be terrified. Is she terrified?"

"No, she is calm. There is something inside her. She trusts the world. I don't want her to lose this trust."

"I would be thinking about my heart all the time."

"You are touching your heart right now."

Marcos's phone buzzed. "Iara," he said, and tapped out a reply.

"I assume she doesn't know I'm here," I said.

He picked up one of the empty bottles.

"Another?"

He went to the counter and returned with two more.

My phone buzzed. Marcos took a drink of the wine while I tapped out a reply to my husband, who was still at work, he said.

Without looking up from my phone I asked where Iara was.

"She's at home with Francesca. She doesn't want Francesca to see her sister like this. She will remember such a thing forever, Iara says."

"Parenthood seems to involve a great deal of lying," I said.

"Children also lie."

"Do you feel guilty?"

"Sometimes the truth is not perfect."

I said, "My husband wants girls, daughters. I find it interesting, the way people have that kind of preference. Did you want girls?"

"No, boys, of course."

"Oh."

"What do you want?"

"I don't. I don't want. And it's the one thing you really cannot disagree about."

My phone buzzed. I replied to my husband. When writing texts, I insisted on punctuation, capitalization, correct syntax; the extra time this required made me hate sending texts. I wished I could stet the errors and not worry, wished I could use the colloquial abbreviations everyone used, my husband used.

"I told him I'm out. I said you're your wife," I said.

"Did he ask what you are doing with Iara?"

"He seemed busy."

"He is," Marcos said.

He looked at his phone.

"Do you know how many e-mails I have not answered today?"

I touched his hand briefly. I didn't know why. I was obeying impulse, in response to a passing feeling I wanted to acknowledge before it vanished.

"I think wanting children requires being innately optimistic about the future," I said.

"That's—"

His phone buzzed against the table.

"I mean—"

The phone buzzed again.

"It's—"

The phone buzzed a third time.

"O meu Deus," Marcos said.

He stood and made a call.

I watched him speaking on the phone, and then I stood, too. He didn't seem to notice. I walked around the back of the café, away from the clack and hiss of the espresso machine. It was almost ten o'clock. The only people in the halls were the night staff, and the only patients were in their beds. No one was coming or going. If you came to the hospital at ten o'clock at night it was by definition an emergency. When I returned to the table, Marcos was there, drinking the wine.

He didn't say anything as I sat down.

"What did Iara want?"

"It wasn't Iara. It was the office."

"An emergency," I said.

"No, it's O.K."

"But somebody needed you."

"Yes."

"Was it a boss or a subordinate? Were you being yelled at or were you the one yelling?"

"It was your husband."

"Oh," I said.

"He wanted advice."

"Advice?"

"About a decision."

"And he had to call you."

"It is a significant decision."

"What did you tell him?"

"I told him he does not have enough information."

"But he has to make the decision tonight?"

"He should."

Marcos drank some wine.

On the T.V. somebody scored a goal, and a crowd cheered.

Marcos said, "I will tell you a story about your husband. A few months ago, one of the men who works with us had a child. But there was a complication. The birth was very difficult for the mother. And so the man, he was out of work, at the hospital with his wife and son, for two or three weeks. During this time, he had a birthday, the new father. Your husband made arrangements for a group of us to go to the hospital, to bring food and gifts, and to spend the afternoon with this man and his family, to make them feel better. This was a very Brazilian thing to do, you know, to behave like this. Your husband was singing, he knew all the words in Portuguese. He was holding the baby. So he was being a good Brazilian, but it made us all very uncomfortable that he was doing this. It is difficult to explain. This is why I don't tell him about Juliana. I am afraid he will do the same thing for me, come here, and I don't want that."

I was silent. The story didn't sound like my husband at all, like any person I knew. My husband hadn't said anything about it.

The T.V. above us was showing news of the protests—the footage was from two days ago, and there were plans for more protests soon, yesterday's news becoming tomorrow's news. I recognized the banners, slogans, buildings, even the faces, it seemed.

Marcos watched for a moment, then said, "The governor's in trouble now for the trains."

"I didn't know."

"Bad contracts on the metro system. Bribes. Millions of reais. Now they protest for this as well."

The café was beginning to close down. The staff were clearing tables and emptying the pastry display.

I already knew that I would remember this night distinctly—it felt already like something I was remembering rather than something I was still in the middle of—but that it was nevertheless a night that had no meaning, that made no difference. My mind traveled over the great, dark quantities of city, the checkerboards of light in the apartment towers, the millions and millions of lives, the small, dark streets named for forgotten councilmen; São Paulo. The women working at the café, the men sweeping the floors, they would all have to go home; they would go home via the wide avenues, down those dark, small streets, the last bus of the night. I wasn't happy and I wasn't unhappy. My favorite word in Portuguese was either *saudade* or *cidade*. I would remember the feeling of being in the hospital at night, on the margins of somebody else's crisis, and the feeling of this time with Marcos, the only time like this I would spend with him. It was the intimacy of knowing that after this night I would see him less and less, and eventually I wouldn't see him at all, since I knew that whatever was happening between us was not in fact happening. It was the feeling of knowing the future but being unable to alter it. It was the pleasure of missing something I never had.

"So this was your idea of a second date," I said.

He smiled.

"Have you had affairs?"

"Well," he said.

"I have a husband. You have a wife."

"But that is not the reason you are hesitating."

"I was very young when I met my husband," I said.

He waited.

I said, "I think about the night my husband and I were robbed by those boys. Then I think, what if Marcos and I were having an affair, and instead of my husband I was with Marcos when those boys robbed us? And I think of everything that would have been even more difficult, all the additional lying, which would only lead to more lying, and so on. And I think I would have reacted differently to the situation if it had been you instead of my husband. I can stand being disappointed by my husband, because he is my husband, but I doubt I could stand being disappointed by a man I was only sleeping with, because then what's the point."

Marcos listened to this, and then was silent.

"No, I don't think that is what would happen," he said at last. And then he laughed.

"Let's go check on your daughter," I said.

We took the wine with us. Juliana was still asleep. She was going to be O.K., according to the doctors, according to Marcos. She was a beautiful child. In obvious ways she resembled both Marcos and Iara, who were beautiful parents.

"You are not supposed to say these things," he said, "but I love Juliana the most. I see myself in her."

Marcos stood away from the bed now. I recalled the moment, earlier, when he touched his daughter's foot through the blanket. I had started to see everything in life as performative, every act a possible performance for a possible audience—believing that we only do what we do with the possibility in mind of an audience seeing it—and yet here was something, the father touching his daughter's foot, that was plainly not a performance, rather an act done out of deep need. He was answering a bolt of feeling. The love for a child was something completely distinct from the love for a spouse. I went to the girl in the bed and touched her foot through the blanket. When I took away my hand, I looked to Marcos, but he had his back to me.

I said, "How did you decide on the name Juliana?"

"A name we liked. Francesca was the same. There is no family meaning."

"It must be so painful."

"They give her drugs. But the drugs are another difficulty. You see how small she is. She is strong."

Marcos's phone buzzed.

"We want to make a normal life for her. So we don't talk about it. You know what I think? If we were, you know, bad people, if we hit her, or something like this—it would not be any worse. This is already the worst that is possible. And this is our fault. She is born this way only because we have decided to make her."

"You're wrong," I said. "It is not the same as if you mistreated her."

His phone buzzed again.

"It is not the same thing because she knows she is loved," I said.

"Iara is certain she will hate us. Because she will have this all her life. For her, the future is like this. It...difficults our marriage."

My phone buzzed.

"I know this is not good English," he said. "But in Portuguese *difficult* can be a verb also."

"You're angry," I said.

"There is no one to be angry to."

"People get angry with God."

"I don't get angry with God," he said. "That is not the reason for God."

His phone buzzed.

I said, "I have it easy. I don't believe in God."

"I think that is more difficult," he said.

My phone buzzed, and then his phone buzzed.

"It difficults some things more than others," I said.

Marcos was looking at his unconscious daughter.

"Another?" he said.

There was still wine in my cup.

My phone buzzed.

"Two's enough," I said.

I looked at my husband's texts. He was finally leaving work.

"I should go home," I said.

Marcos nodded. His phone buzzed.

"I'll finish your wine," he said.

That night, in bed with my husband, drowsy, loving, games of talk.

"Jazz singers."

"O.K.," I said.

"Billie."

"Nina."

"Sarah."

"Ella."

"Dinah."

"Ella. That's the one."

RETURN

This happens later, in Lisbon. I'm standing at a little bar, open to the square, and one of the men there sells me a ginjinha, the cherry brandy special to this part of Portugal. Patrons linger—men, all of them men—having a drink, then another. I am a woman by herself, and so they look at me a certain way. I drink a little of the liqueur and chew the fruit that sits at the bottom. I don't like the taste, I knew I wouldn't, it is too sweet, but all the guidebooks mention the ginjinha, to the point that it seems like bad manners not to try it. And a sip won't hurt. This is the future, but everything around me is the same as it was years ago, down to the men selling cherry brandy on the square—that's the charm of a city like Lisbon, where change takes so long to arrive. There is always comfort in knowing that something hasn't changed. The air is pleasant, cool. Today, after meetings, I almost decided to go back to the hotel to sleep; instead, with the afternoon free, I took the train out to the suburb of Belém, on the Tagus River. There I saw the Padrão dos Descobrimentos. Salazar ordered it built as a tribute to Portugal's history of exploration and empire, just as that history was coming to an end. I stared for a long time, as tourists came and went, taking pictures with their phones. It is a really hideous, fascistic thing, ugly and weathered with age, yet somehow moving. At the base of the monument, there are statues of Portuguese explorers, men who left home and sailed to Africa and Asia and America. There is Henry the Navigator, and Pedro Álvares Cabral, who discovered Brazil. Their stone bodies ascend a kind of ramp, as if they're all preparing to dive into the Tagus. I was struck by the visual echo of the Monumento às Bandeiras in São Paulo: the concrete bandeirantes march toward destiny in a similar way. It, too, commemorates an act of exploration. The bandeirantes—pioneers, the men who opened the Brazilian interior. They hacked through jungle and warred with Indians and died of disease. Exploration is a strange impulse, one I used to think of as essentially male, something in the wiring that compels a man to depart rather than remain and improve the place where he is. A long time ago, a male friend, who was also studying anthropology, said to me that when a man goes to a place where he looks different from the natives, he can be sure of two things: the women will want to sleep with him and the men will want to kill him. Sex with unusual women must be worth the risk, I'd replied. I spent the rest of the afternoon in Belém—visiting the Saint Jerome monastery, the old military tower, eating the local pastry with its dense white heart of cream—and thought of the young Portuguese sailors who, centuries before, had set out from this place on the mouth of the Tagus. Inside the monastery was Vasco da Gama's tomb. He had died in India; his remains were returned to Portugal years later. Now he lay in effigy, in white marble, palms joined in prayer. How strange that so long after his death the remains of one of the world's most famous explorers were repatriated out of a belief that no matter where he has been in life a man should lie forever in the place where he was born. Now that I seem to be always on a plane (I am now a person with that sort of job), I admit it pleases me, departure. Departures are always more interesting than returns; but I never think of not returning. Night was falling by the time the train from Belém deposited me back in Lisbon. Lisbon is an attractive place; I liked it at once. Now it's dark. It's time to move on. I throw away the plastic cup with the last of the ginjinha and walk away from the square. I want to wander a little in the streets. I listen for something warm, familiar—music coming from a bar, the noise of conversation in a restaurant. Nothing. Portugal is famous for fado music, but it's hard to find it performed anywhere, it seems; you bring an idea to a country when you visit. At last I come across a café. I sit and ask for tea—*chá*, a word I remember. Another customer looks at me, but he doesn't say anything. A group of young Portuguese men and women talk animatedly, huddled around a table, students, maybe. All day I have been surrounded by the Portuguese language, and surely this is the reason for the memories of Brazil that have surfaced. The Portuguese in Portugal is different from the Portuguese of Brazil, but I am happy to listen to it; to my ear it's a friendly sound. The flight home is tomorrow. I'm a little disappointed already at the thought of returning to America; I find myself restless when I'm there. It's difficult to care about the politics, the T.V. shows, the things people want to talk about. Without thinking, I use the word *home* to refer to the hotel in a city where I'm spending a few nights as easily as I use it to refer to the apartment where I live. Home is everywhere and nowhere; there's no weight left in the word for me. We rent an apartment and in not so long we will rent a different apartment. I understand this is a privileged kind of displacement. I have a home; I have good reasons to return there. I know how serious the word *home* is for other people. At breakfast that morning I saw footage on CNN of the refugees who have come into Greece, Hungary, Serbia, the same continent where I now drink tea in a quiet café. On the flight from Newark to Lisbon, I read an article in the *New Yorker* about a man who fled from Syria to Lebanon, then Turkey, Greece, Macedonia, and then through Hungary to Austria, Germany, and finally Sweden. His journey was terrible, his circumstances, but, instead of feeling sympathy for him, I was angry, because he left his wife behind. She was to follow him once he was settled, to make the journey alone. He lives in Gothenburg now, cashing benefits checks from the Swedish government, while his wife listens to bombs falling over Damascus. This seems to me unforgivable; but surely I'm not in a position to say. I pay for the tea and go. I get a little lost, things aren't quite what I remember; eventually I find my way. I was ready to head home—back to the hotel, I mean—but now the pleasure of walking, of solitude, seizes me again, and I slow down, almost involuntarily. Soon enough I'll be forbidden from traveling, at least for a while; I don't know the next time I'll have a moment like this to savor. Once upon a time America represented the ends of the earth, virgin territory, a place that men like Vasco da Gama dreamed of. Now from almost every corner of the globe you can take a nonstop flight to New York. "I hate traveling and explorers," wrote Lévi-Strauss at the beginning of *Tristes Tropiques*. In Brazil, the protests are starting again, a new wave of protests; people's anger is not yet exhausted. The president seems to be headed for impeachment. Some Brazilians even say they want the return of military dictatorship. The world is filled with unthinkable things. I put a hand on my stomach; I am always doing that now; another cliché. *Now that we have this*. I turn a corner and see the hotel—I'm here. For a moment, I stand motionless on this street in an unfamiliar city, and then I continue toward the hotel doors, because it is late already, and he is at home, waiting for me to call, wondering where I am.

SYMPATHY FOR THE WIFE

I stood at the window and watched the unsteady burning of city lights, the quiet streets, my reflection printed on black glass. This wasn't the past and it wasn't the future; this was São Paulo. The apartment was my apartment, our apartment; this was home. Planes, coming down through night, were suddenly at eye level with buildings, a controlled violence of metal and gears that from where I was standing looked like floating, like grace.

We have to live in the time we live in. Is there anyone—and I include myself—who doesn't suffer the pangs of era anxiety, a feeling of being born at the wrong moment? My husband—my husband suffered no anxiety. He was happily in and of his time. He liked his Kindle Voyage, his Galaxy, his Venture rewards card, the frictionless pleasures of on-demand, the steam baths of Wi-Fi. A life as straightforward as switching to airplane mode, a life in which the important thing was to remember your passwords. I knew this about him when we married. He was consistent. This consistency was inherent to his appeal. I was at the start and for a very long time piercingly in love with him; I had dated my share of aspiring poets and artists, and he was different. He was a dependable creature. When he was unhappy, there was a floor to his unhappiness; he didn't turn gloomy. His emotions were orderly, they didn't swarm. I once imagined that his characterological consistency was something I could participate in, climb into, like a passenger in a sedan with a driver. That he would serve to balance out my not so dependable qualities. I had thought his uncomplicated happiness would make me happy, too.

At a point during my twenties I had stopped questioning the comforts of money. But then something changed; I no longer enjoyed the enjoyment. And so I was seeing the casualties of capitalism everywhere, the forces coming into play, the hidden currents that made my life easier and other people's lives more difficult. I felt: discomfort. Discomfort—it's the easiest political emotion in the world. You can grow comfortable with a lot of discomfort.

Most recent common ancestor refers to the last human being who was a genetic ancestor of all human beings living today. Complex mathematical modeling suggests that this man or woman may have lived between two thousand and five thousand years ago. People are surprised to learn that our most recent common ancestor might have lived within the imaginable past. *Identical ancestors point* refers to the moment in the past when everyone living was either an ancestor of all people alive today or an ancestor of none. This may have been seventy-five thousand years ago. Even that span is such a minor stain on time—dark, mindless time.

Every time I went to the church there were men and women I hadn't seen before. New arrivals, émigrés. Others, whose faces I had come to know, were gone. It was a place of flux. *Émigré*—you only ever hear the term used in reference to the kind of refugee who has a violin case among his baggage; it has a connotation of nobility salvaged from disaster. I saw a man sitting on the floor, against the wall, opening an orange with his thumbnail. Two women were with him, one on each side, falling against his shoulders. The man ate the orange and, with the other hand, started texting on his mobile phone, its charger still plugged into the wall. I asked who he was texting. "La famille," he said. Was one of the women his wife? Were they his sisters? "Non," he said.

Padre Piero and I spoke with two brothers, Syrian. One had some English, and one had some French; a conversation of shards. Now and then the brothers consulted in Arabic, the father and I in Portuguese. They had a contact in São Paulo, a distant cousin, maybe. They wanted advice about papers. Every other sentence would begin: "Dans la guerre..." They were educated; one had been a medical student before the war. Their father was dead. It was becoming both more dangerous to leave and more dangerous to stay, they said. They had flown to Istanbul, and from there to São Paulo, a journey that marked them as lucky. They said they would never go back; they said eventually everyone was going to leave Syria. Everyone they knew was talking about Europe. They knew people who were talking about crossing the sea. It is so bad you will die to leave, they said. I listened and nodded. There was nothing to say. The future wasn't supposed to look like this.

The protests were petering out. I had no news of Luciano. Claudia had dropped me as a tutor, or I had dropped her as a client; I'd dropped most of my clients. Everything was petering out. First it was about the twenty-centavo increase in the bus fare, and then it was about the insult of the transportation system generally, and then it was about the shoddy conditions of all public services, and the waste of public money, and the corruption of politicians, and the failure of institutions, and then it seemed to be about the sheer fact of politics, and then no one was sure what it was about. Autumn was coming, except it was really spring. It turns out you can't protest everything at once.

We met at a party, Manhattan, someone's apartment. He mixed us something with gin, and we got a little tipsy. This was a time when I still took moral instruction from the literature I read. I made a remark to the effect that Joan Didion was my favorite writer. I was embarrassed to have spoken in earnest. I told him it made me feel like a cliché to have the same favorite writer as so many other women like me. It felt like a choice of scarf. I said I thought Joan Didion's collected essays were the Great American Novel. On our second date, I wouldn't kiss him, but squeezed his hand to say good night, long enough to let him know what I was feeling, and only then did I realize how warm my palms were. They were sweating, I was so nervous.

Somebody a while ago pulled a stunt by submitting *Pride and Prejudice* to a publisher; the publisher rejected it. Proving what? Proving that Jane Austen wouldn't write like that if she were alive today.

Once upon a time I dated a poet who didn't own a bed. He slept on a mattress on the floor, in a half bedroom near Myrtle Avenue, and paid minimal, under-the-table rent to the friend whose name was on the lease. "It's interesting as a white man to live in a neighborhood where you're the minority," the poet told me.

The man who would become my husband was a finance guy who read Joan Didion. If you haven't dated in New York City you have no idea how rare that is. He was handsome, and charming, and he wasn't insecure. He wasn't nearly as well-read as the poet who didn't own a bed, but he owned a bed; and, after more than one guy like the poet who didn't own a bed, I believed that the man who would become my husband was what I wanted. No—I didn't merely believe it. I was twenty-three. I wanted him so fucking much.

What I thought was a protest in our neighborhood turned out to be a religious procession. I went out to the balcony when I heard the sounds. It was evening. Several hundred people with candles in their hands moved slowly up our street, a street called Divine Savior, as a priest in ordinary clothes issued promises of God's love through a megaphone, and two men played acoustic guitars while a woman sang a beautiful, haunting melody. We watched from the balcony, and saw our neighbors also watching from their balconies. They filmed the performance with their smartphones. I wondered if the parishioners thought of the procession as a performance. I asked my husband what the occasion was. On the Internet he learned that it was the feast day of Our Lady of Aparecida, the patron saint of Brazil, for whom our neighborhood's church was named. Nossa Senhora da Conceição Aparecida was the name given to a statue of the Madonna fished out of a river—a statue of a Black Madonna, in fact, said my husband, now reporting from Wikipedia—by three fishermen in a small village north of São Paulo, in 1717, as they prepared a meal to honor the visiting governor.

The statue's race was politically convenient in a country whose poor were descended from Africans. Local people gave the statue credit for a miracle performed on behalf of a young slave, and then they built a church nearby. From there the myth accelerated—my husband found more about the statue, as I read the screen over his shoulder, no longer watching the slow candlelight procession in the street, which really had been quite beautiful, the candlelight in the parishioners' hands a surprisingly tender sight to behold. I subscribed instantly to the factuality of everything I was reading, even though it was written anonymously and described events in rural Brazil three hundred years ago, probably documented only sketchily even at the time. My husband scrolled down. Popes made decrees about the statue and its importance; the government declared a national holiday in the statue's honor—if you want people to believe in something, give them a day off from work. The songs of the parishioners in the street reached the sixteenth floor and floated in through open windows, the voice of the priest from the megaphone. In 1980, Pope John Paul II came all the way from Rome to visit Aparecida—as the town inevitably became known—and to consecrate the church there as a minor basilica.

If I was thinking a lot in those days about the nature of time, the seemingly constant interpenetration of eras, a sense of time not as linear but as a confusion of folds, it was because I was at that point engaged in an excavation of my own past. Of, specifically, the past with my husband, my husband who now wanted a child, who always wanted a child, with whom I argued because I could not decide if I wanted a child. Memories surfaced. When a memory made me happy, I felt pain. For instance, the charm of my husband's smile when we first met. It was the same smile he had now and it also wasn't the same smile he had now: both statements were true. Although it was possible that I was transferring the image of his smile now onto the memory of him at a party in Manhattan years ago, at a time when I didn't even know his last name; that more recent memories had overwritten older ones. It wasn't as simple as saying that we were happy and then we weren't. The early days, the middle years, of our relationship seemed to coexist with the different, more difficult situation we had now, they were folded in, and this made the situation even more troubled than it already was; I would open a newspaper in Brazil and read about a demonstration by an indigenous-rights group that turned ugly when men with painted faces shot arrows at policemen armed with semiautomatic weapons.

I stood at the window and watched the burning of city lights, the activity at the corner bar, the jets coming in for landing, the blue street signs hanging at intersections, the somber apartment towers. A city finds its most perfect expression at night; the lights are a proof of life. I heard the latch turn, my husband undoing the locks. Then he was standing behind me: I saw him as a reflection alongside my reflection, ghosts upon the city's illumination. "I thought you were working late," I said. "I thought so, too," he said.

Helen wrote with news that she was seeing someone:

> So. I am officially through the looking-glass of the first person plural. I say, "Oh, we enjoyed that movie." It's unnerving: I've never done that before. He works for the State Department, and in a year he's moving to Madrid. Doesn't that sound like fun. His Spanish is already very good. Vamanos.

We attended a performance by a German string quartet at the Centro Cultural. It was free. They played Schubert, *Death and the Maiden*. I forgot everything around me as they performed. Schubert has a depth, a velvet luxury, that nothing else quite matches. When the music ended, I took my husband's hand. He turned to me. I could see that he had been lost as well. Nothing was so powerful as art.

I used to imagine that I could have a life made of art. I never wanted to be an artist, but believed I could have this ancillary thing, the life made of art. I had misread signs. I had made wrong estimates—of time, of other people, of myself. You could diagnose my problem as an affliction of vagueness: *a life made of art*. I didn't know what it meant when I was younger, and I don't know now.

Helen:

> What's become clear to me is that all dating is repetition. The fun parts and the shitty parts. The part where you tell somebody about yourself, discuss food preferences, allergies, talk about fucking *Game of Thrones*—it's hideous. It's like one of those video games where you die and start over, except every time you start over you're older. I used to think of monogamy as the opposite of experience, the enemy of healthy variety, but now I see that I was wrong. It's dating that's monotonous. Every first date is the same: it's either a bad one or a good one. All men fuck you the same way. I want

to see what happens when I get past the parts I already know.

So. My husband was being transferred back to New York. He made it sound like the normal course of things; but I knew something had happened that he was trying to downplay. I asked, gently, a day or so later. "I was holding the wrong position," he said. "A bet. A big bet. Two, actually, two related bets." He added, "It cost a lot to bring us here"; he meant for the bank. "What did Marcos say?" I asked. He looked at me strangely: "Why Marcos?" "He's the only co-worker of yours I know," I said. He was going back to New York. We were going back to New York. I was going back to New York.

This was, as it always is, somebody else's script, written long ago, acted out already countless times. The past anticipates the future, or the future plagiarizes the past, one or the other, or both.

The country would never be the same after the protests; everything was going to be different now. Or else the protests had come to nothing and nothing would change. The opinion writers were having it both ways. A judge ordered the release from prison of high-ranking politicians convicted of bribery, pending appeals. A cloth soaked in vinegar would protect you from tear gas. Information began to accumulate. Hundreds of people in Lapa waited in line ten hours to buy monthly bus passes. In the River of January, the military police were pacifying the favelas.

You and I makes we. He and I also makes we. We can easily become ambiguous. This hadn't seemed like a problem before.

For my husband it was a time of personal crisis. His customary professional certainty was invaded by doubt. I wanted to comfort him. I didn't want to miss the opportunity to comfort him. I wouldn't have wanted to do that for anyone else, want so absolutely to be there for a moment of personal disaster. With anyone else, I wouldn't have felt as though I would be missing out if I were absent during an unhappy time. I wanted to act in defense of this life, our life. I thought: If, in the end, we are together, all this will become a part of the story we tell ourselves about our marriage. I thought: A marriage is built on nothing so much as the story of that marriage. It felt as though I had come to the conclusion of a mathematical proof. And then I thought: Marriage is also a thing that happens inside your own head.

Mariology refers to the systematic study within the Catholic Church of the person and nature of Mary. We're talking about centuries of effort to make sense of a single woman. The findings of the mariologists—men, you have to assume—are one source of the church's infallible doctrine.

Another interest of mine is words that have no descendants. There are words that aren't really the roots of anything—*anagnostes*, *bucaeda*. They are words that once appeared in the

Roman vocabulary and then went out of use. They never evolved, never produced word children, at least not in English. And so they seem strange to us now. A word like *latebricola* sounds especially alien to the twenty-first-century ear.

Who remembers being a child? When you unhesitatingly touched the bark of a tree, because you had to know how it felt. When you lay on grass and hard dirt, facedown and peaceful, both hands pressed against the body of the earth, after running around for a while, and thought to yourself how solid and permanent it all seemed. Adulthood is less sensory, I think. I still look, but I don't touch, or I don't as much.

A gauze of pale light stretched around buildings after the rain. It was a city of liquor bottles, soccer matches, cheap motorcycles, boys in the road, businessmen. Sometimes it was beautiful.

Toward the end of a dismal time in Naples trying to sell a piece of family property, the English couple in Rossellini's *Journey to Italy*, on the precipice of divorce, embrace passionately after they become separated amid the fever of a Catholic religious procession. The need they feel for one another in that moment is plainly the consequence of panic in an unfamiliar foreign place—the same foreign place that, for the entire film, they have blamed for exposing the flaws in their marriage. They embrace out of fear, in other words, not devotion. At least that's how I always saw it. I've watched it more than once. The husband is cruel, even brutish. He aspires to philander. The wife is sensitive, accommodating, intelligent. They tack between boredom and hostility. The wife's dilemma seems to be a lack of self-knowledge, unless it's too much self-knowledge. Rossellini, a man, appeared to have more sympathy for the wife, played by his own wife, Ingrid Bergman. But I can't sympathize at all: the decision to embrace her husband at the end has always bothered me. It is obvious—or it was obvious to me when I first saw the film—that within days, even hours, they will begin to argue again. Their embrace is merely the postponement of something difficult; or it is confirmation that the wife doesn't know how to escape a life of unhappiness. Apparently some people don't see it this way—they see it as the miraculous return of love. That surprises me. I never thought it was supposed to be a happy ending. So.

ACKNOWLEDGMENTS

My thanks to Max Goldberg, Peter Lord, and Uzo Iweala for careful readings and thoughtful criticism, and to Anna Stein and Carina Guiterman, who made a place in the world for this book.